哈福

每天 5分鐘

流利英語一本通

施孝昌◎著 附 MP3

5種感覺學英語，5倍速暢說英語

哈福

5 種感覺學英語，5 倍速暢說英語

　　5 分鐘學好英語的秘訣，就是運用人的 5 種感知系統，聽說觸看聞，完全開發右腦潛能，5 感全開發、5 種感覺學英語、5 倍速暢說英語、5 倍速學會英語會話。亦即 1 倍用聽的：耳聽老師講解文法，2 倍用說的：口說三段式會話，3 倍用觸的：手觸超語感句型，4 倍用看的：放眼望單字，5 倍用聞的：嗅出慣用語。

Then.....

Your English will be excellent!

　　一般人學習英語十幾年，還不會應用，不敢開口，本書讓您信心重整，在短期內發揮潛力十足，一舉成功。英語學習也沒有年齡限制，何時起步，都不嫌晚，五十歲才立志學習而一舉成功的大有人在。國中、高中、甚至大學，往往因為年紀較小，無法體會「英語」的重要性，成年後因應需要，決心加上「竅門」，必然很快就能說上一口流利的英語。

　　本書與眾不同之處，是利用平日最熟悉的日常會話，讓大家「自然學會」動詞的運用。用最簡單淺顯的重點，分析解說，並加以活用，讓您迅速掌握英語的學習核心，只要有中學的英文程度，就能輕輕鬆鬆學好動詞的各種時態變化。

　　本書收集了 60 個動詞時態變化的基礎句型，您只要

記住它，有關動詞的時態變化立可精通。如此一來，無論考試、求職、晉升或與老外聊天，您都可以行遍天下無敵手。

　　不知道您是否記得，在您的孩堤時代牙牙學語時，最先學會的，是那些詞句呢？是不是肚子餓了，想「吃」東西？口渴了，想「喝」水？還是累了，想「睡覺」？長大一點，就常說「我要上學」、「我想出去玩」、或常跟媽媽提到「我們老師說…」？

　　沒錯，不管任何一種語言，「動詞」正是學會該語言的精華所在。因為它可以單純、直接地表達人類的欲望、意識、及想法。而中文和英文最大的差異，也在於「動詞」的運用。而華人在學英文時，之所以對「動詞」感到困擾，原因在於英文的動詞有「主被動」、「時態」、「第三人稱」的變化。意思是，英文的動詞變化，會因為主詞、或發生的時間而改變，所以這種「動詞用法」也相對較中文複雜難懂。

　　但反過來說，如果能掌握原則，把「動詞用法」這個關節打通，就好像打通語言的任督二脈，語感隨著動詞的輪轉，活絡全身，像說中文一般，準確、直覺地表達意思，順暢地脫口而出！

Contents

第 3 章　用英語操縱對方的秘訣 -Will

第4章　如何正確表達事件的時間

第 5 章　完成式在會話的應用

目
錄

第 6 章　大膽的假設

第 7 章　英語會話常用被動式

第8章　英語會話慣用法

第 1 章

最簡單的
英語表達法

1.1 It's eight o'clock.

現在已經八點了

MP3
02

　　不是英美語系國家的人說英語,最容易犯的錯誤是化簡為繁。也就是說,原本很簡單可以表達的一句話,卻說得很複雜,弄得沒人能理解他到底在說什麼。本課要學的重點就是如何簡單地提醒時間「已經」到了。

　　很多人說英語時,一想到「已經」,就有想用「現在完成式」——「have+ 過去分詞」的衝動,實際上,你看我們的標題,「已經八點」只要簡單說 It's eight o'clock. 就行了,在正確的英語會話裡,甚至連把 It 和 is 分開來說都嫌太麻煩,直接連起來說成 It's 才自然。請

注意聽 MP3 老師的示範。

　　「句型練習」裡的例句雖然有讚美的話、有問句、有請求,但每句話都是關於一件很平常的事實,所以都只要簡單地用現在式來表達就可以了。

對話一

☺ M: It's eight o'clock.
　　現在已經八點。

We are late for dinner.
我們晚餐要遲到了。

☺ W: What are you talking about?

你在說什麼呢？

☺ M: We are supposed to have diner with John tonight.

今天晚上我們約好跟約翰一起吃晚飯的。

☺ W: That's right.

對啊！

I totally forgot.

我完全忘了。

☺ M: We had better get going.

我們最好得快點走。

對話二

☺ M: Are you going to vote this week?

這個禮拜你會去投票嗎？

☺ W: I'm not sure.

我還不確定。

☺ M: Why not?

為何不確定？

☺ W: I am having a hard time deciding between the two candidates.

在這兩個候選人當中我不知道怎麼做決定。

☺ M: I will be happy to share my opinions if you want.

如果妳願意的話，我很樂意把我的看法告訴妳。

對話三

☺ M: John, do you know what you are scheduled to talk about tonight?

約翰，你知道你今天晚上預定要講些什麼嗎？

☺ W: As far as I know, I am talking about fourth quarter earnings.

據我所知，我要談的是第四季的利潤。

☺ M: Yes, but you're also supposed to talk about the increase in the stock value.

對，不過你也得要談談有關股價增值的事。

☺ W: I guess I had better get some information ready then.

那麼，我想我最好要把一些資料準備好。

☺ M: That would be a good idea.

那是個好主意。

句型練習

❶ Those shoes are nice. Are they new?

那雙鞋子很好看。是新的嗎？

❷ John isn't interested in politics.

約翰對政治沒有興趣。

❸ Can you close the windows, please? I'm cold.

可以請你把窗戶關上嗎？我會冷。

❹ I'm sure glad we're not at that crowded movie theater.

我好慶幸我們沒在那間擁擠的電影院。

❺ Cars are expensive in my country.

在我的國家，汽車是很貴的。

基礎單字

☺ **vote**		投票
☺ **candidate** [ˈkændəˌdet]		候選人
☺ **share** [ʃɛr]		分享
☺ **opinion** [əˈpɪnjən]		意見
☺ **forgot**		忘記
☺ **quarter** [ˈkwɔrtɚ]		一季（三個月）
☺ **increase** [ˈɪnkris]		增加
☺ **earnings** [ˈɝnɪŋz]		利潤
☺ **stock**		股票
☺ **value**		價值
☺ **information** [ˌɪnfɚˈmeʃən]		資料
☺ **politics** [ˈpɑləˌtɪks]		政治

☺ **conference** [ˈkɑnfərəns]	研討會
☺ **crowded** [ˈkraʊdɪd]	擁擠的

慣用語

☺ **be supposed to**	應當要
☺ **be scheduled to**	排定好
☺ **had better**	最好
☺ **movie theater**	戲院
☺ **be late for ～**	遲到

2 Most stores close at 11:00 p.m.

大多數商店在晚上十一點打烊

MP3 03

在做英語會話交談的時候，很多人會一面講話，一面思索中學老師所教的文法規則，深怕出錯，結果是越怕越錯。你彷彿記得老師曾經說過，英文句子中若是有指

定時間的話，要依這個時間是「過去」的時間，還是「未來的」時間，來決定要用「過去式」或「未來式」。你看我們的標題：雖然句子中有指定「晚上十一點」的時間，但動詞還是僅用一個最簡單的 close 而已，根本無所謂現在式或未來式。其實商店定時打烊是天天要做的事，是一種很普通的習慣，所以用簡單的現在式就行，講英語時不要想太多，免得反倒阻礙了你的思路。

注意體會「句型練習」中每一個例句所表達的意思，再詳細揣摩如何將這些意思正確用英語表達出來，你是不是可以歸納出來，英語會話其實真的很簡單？

☺ M: I hear that most stores here close at 11:00p.m.

我聽說這裡大多數商店都在晚上十一點打烊。

☺ W: Actually, they close at 9:00 p.m.

事實上，他們是晚上九點就關門。

☺ M: I wonder why John said 11:00 p.m.

我不知道為什麼約翰說是晚上十一點。

☺ W: They close at 11:00 p.m. around holiday times.

在放假日期間，他們是晚上十一點打烊。

☺ M: Oh, I heard him wrong then.

哦，那麼是我聽錯了。

☺ M: We need to buy Tom a birthday present today.

我們今天需要給湯姆買一份生日禮物。

☺ W: Where should we go to find one?

我們要到哪裡去買呢？

☺ M: I think the best place is the mall.

我認為最好的地方是在大型購物中心。

☺ W: The mall is very crowded on weekends.

週末時大型購物中心非常擁擠的。

☺ M: I know. That's why we are leaving right after breakfast.

我知道，那就是為什麼我們吃過早餐後馬上就得走。

對話三

☺ M: I always have trouble with this jar of jelly.

我總是沒辦法打開這種果醬罐子。

☺ W: Here, I can open it for you.

來，我可以幫你打開。

☺ M: Thanks, what is the trick?

謝謝你，有什麼竅門沒有？

☺ W: The lid is sticky from the jelly.

這個蓋子因為果醬而變得很黏。

So I pop the lid up with a spoon.

所以我就用湯匙敲開蓋子。

☺ M: Good. Now I don't have to bother you with it.

好。這樣我就不用再麻煩你了。

☺ W: Yes, but it is no bother at all.

好啊，不過那並不算麻煩的。

❶ It is hot today.

今天好熱噢！

❷ Without a ticket, you cannot get on the bus.

沒有車票，你不能上公車。

❸ I need three volunteers to help me on this project.

我需要三個義工來幫我做這個專案。

❹ The phone bill is high this month.

這個月的電話費好高噢！

❺ The guest house is in bad shape.

客房的情況很不好。

基礎單字

✿ **present** [ˈprɛzn̩t]		禮物
✿ **find**		找到
✿ **mall** [mɔl]		大型購物中心
✿ **weekend**		週末
✿ **close**		關門
✿ **holiday** [ˈhɑləde]		假期
✿ **wrong** [rɔŋ]		錯誤的

trouble [ˈtrʌbḷ]	困難
jar [dʒɑr]	罐子
jelly [ˈdʒɛlɪ]	果醬
trick [trɪk]	竅門
lid	蓋子
spoon [spun]	湯匙
sticky [ˈstɪkɪ]	黏的
bother	麻煩
project [ˈprɑdʒɛkt]	專案；企畫
volunteer [ˌvɑlənˈtɪr]	義工；志願者

慣用語

get on the bus	上公車
phone bill	電話費
guest house	客房
in bad shape	情況不好
pop something up	撬開某物

3

Mary doesn't go out very often.

瑪莉不常出門

MP3
04

還記得上一課說過，關於一件普通習慣的英語會話，只要簡單地用現在式來表達就行嗎？有時候這種「習慣」是一種說話時的感覺，沒有特別的字眼來暗示，但有時候，講話時的用字已經很明白地顯示所敘述的事是一件經常發生的事，像 often 經常就是一個很明確的字，其他像 all the time 老是，等也都有「經常」的含意，一樣用簡單式就可以了。

　　「句型練習」例句二：I don't have the time. 是「我沒戴手錶，不知道現在是幾點。」的意思，the time 指的是「現在的時刻」，不是指「空閒的時間」，注意 I don't have the time. 與 I don't have time. 我沒空的不同。

對話一

☺ M: How is your aunt doing?

你姨媽怎麼樣了？

☺ W: I guess she is OK.

我猜她還好吧。

☺ M: Why do you say that?

你怎麼這麼說呢？

☺ W: She doesn't go out very often.

她不常出門。

☺ M: Is that bad?

那不好嗎？

☺ W: It just doesn't seem healthy to stay in one place all the time.

老是待在一個地方，似乎是不太健康的。

對話二

☺ M: Have you seen the hammer?

妳看見鐵鎚沒有？

☺ W: No, I have not seen it for weeks.

沒有，我已經好幾星期沒見到它了。

☺ M: Well, I can't find it either.

嗯，我也找不到。

☺ W: I don't have any idea where it could be.

我不知道它會在哪裡。

☺ M: I do not want to buy a new one.

我可不想再買一把新的。

☺ W: Don't worry.

別擔心。

I can find it.

我會找得到的。

☺ M: Where is John?

約翰在哪裡？

☺ W: I don't know.

我不知道。

☺ M: I can't believe that he is late again.

我真不相信他又遲到了。

☺ W: It is not totally his fault.

那也不完全是他的錯。

☺ M: Why not?

怎麼不是？

☺ W: He has to wait for Tom to pick him up.

他得要等湯姆去接他。

句型練習

❶ I can't go out tonight.

今天晚上我不能出去。

❷ I don't have the time.

我不知道現在幾點。

❸ I can not understand why he is always late.
我不懂他為什麼總是遲到。

❹ We are not able to wait any longer.
我們不能再繼續等了。

❺ I am not a fan of country music.
我不是一個鄉村音樂迷。

基礎單字

✿ **aunt** [ænt]	姨媽
✿ **guess**	猜想
✿ **healthy** [ˈhɛlθɪ]	健康的
✿ **often** [ˈɔfən]	時常
✿ **hammer**	鐵鎚
✿ **fault** [fɔlt]	過錯
✿ **country** [ˈkʌntrɪ]	鄉村的
✿ **music**	音樂
✿ **fan**	狂熱愛好者

慣用語

✿ **all the time**	總是
✿ **pick up**	到某地去接人
✿ **country music**	美國鄉村音樂

4 Do you speak English?

你會說英語嗎?

MP3
05

　一個人所具備的能力,例如會說英語、會騎自行車、會用電腦等,都是該人隨時隨地具備的,沒有時間的前後分別,所以在英語會話裡,提到這類的能力問題,也只要用簡單的現在式就對了。

對話一

☺ M: Excuse me, do you speak English?

對不起,你會說英語嗎?

☺ W: Yes, I do.

會,我會。

☺ M: Can you tell me where a bank is?

你可以告訴我哪裡有銀行嗎?

☺ W: I am sorry, but I am not from around here.

很抱歉,我不是這附近的人。

☺ M: Thanks.

謝謝。

I can ask someone else.

我會問其他的人。

對話二

☺ M: Do you work here?

你是這裡的職員嗎？

☺ W: Yes. What can I do for you?

是的。可以為您服務嗎？

☺ M: I am looking for a gift for a friend at the office.

我想找禮物送給我辦公室裡的同事。

☺ W: Can you give me more information?

你能夠說得更詳細一點嗎？

☺ M: She wants some kind of desk calendar.

她想要那種放在桌子上的日曆。

☺ W: We have several different types on aisle seven.

我們有好幾種不同的型式在第七排貨架上。

對話三

☺ M: Can I help you with that?

你要我幫你的忙嗎？

☺ W: No, it is a one man project.

沒辦法，這是只有一個人能做的企劃。

☺ M: Okay, but I am happy to help.

好吧，但我是很樂意幫忙的。

☺ W: Thanks, but everything is really okay.

謝謝你，但是真的沒有問題。

① Is that your hat?
那是你的帽子嗎？

② Can I borrow your ruler?
我可以借用你的尺嗎？

③ Do you know Mary?
妳認識瑪莉嗎？

④ Are you hot, or is it just me?
妳覺得熱嗎？或是只有我覺得熱？

⑤ Can you cook well?
妳很會做菜嗎？

基礎單字

✪ **bank**	銀行
✪ **gift**	禮物
✪ **calendar** [ˈkæləndɚ]	日曆
✪ **aisle** [aɪl]	貨架的行列
✪ **different** [ˈdɪfərənt]	不同的
✪ **cook**	煮飯；做菜
✪ **ruler**	尺

慣用語

✪ **desk calendar**	桌曆

5 What time does the movie begin?

電影什麼時候開演？

MP3 06

我們日常與人溝通，就是一種彼此間的資訊交換，所以用到問句的形式特別多，特別是英語會話，一問一答的機會更多，因此對於問句的徹底理解與應用也就特別重要。

一般的英語會話裡，單純詢問對方某種資訊，例如何時、何地、有什麼事等這樣的問話，與該事情的實際發生並無關係。像標題「電影什麼時候開演？」，只是問開演的時間，而沒有牽涉電影是不是已經、或還沒開演，所以與過去、未來都沒有關係，於是用最簡單的現在式就可以了。

對話一

☺ M: What time does the movie begin?
電影什麼時候開演？

☺ W: It starts at 9:15 p.m.
晚上九點十五分開始。

☺ M: It is already 9:00 p.m.
現在已經九點了。

☺ W: You are right.
你說的對。

We need to get going.

我們得趕快走。

☺ M: Well, I am ready when you are.

嗯，我都準備好了，妳好了就可以走。。

對話二

☺ M: Do you think it is going to rain?

你想會下雨嗎？

☺ W: I don't know.

我不知道。

The weather report says no.

氣象報告說不會。

☺ M: I rarely rely on the weather report.

我很少信賴氣象報告的。

☺ W: They are usually right these days.

近來他們的預告一般都很正確。

☺ M: Yes, technology is always improving.

是的，科技總是在改進的。

對話三

☺ M: I cannot wait for the weekend.

我等不及週末快點到。

☺ W: Why, what are you doing?

為什麼，你有什麼事要做嗎？

☺ M: I plan to go to the lake with the kids.

我計劃帶小孩到湖邊玩。

☺ W: That sounds like a lot of fun.

那聽起來很有趣。

☺ M: I think that it will be.

我想應該是。

句型練習

❶ Do you think the report will be done in time?

你想這份報告可以及時做完嗎？

❷ How far off is his birthday?

距離他的生日還有多久？

❸ When do you plan to move?

你計劃什麼時候搬家？

❹ Can you tell me what time you will be home?

你能告訴我你幾點會在家嗎？

❺ When do we start the meeting?

我們幾點開始開會？

✿ **rain**	下雨
✿ **rely** [rɪˈlaɪ]	倚賴
✿ **usually** [ˈjuʒʊəlɪ]	通常
✿ **weather** [ˈwɛðɚ]	天氣
✿ **report** [rɪˈport]	報告
✿ **technology** [tɛkˈnɑlədʒɪ]	科技
✿ **improving** [ɪmˈpruvɪŋ]	改善的
✿ **meeting**	會議

慣用語

✿ **rely on**	倚賴
✿ **weather report**	氣象報告

第 2 章

用進行式
說出純正英語

6 I am talking with a client.

我正在跟一個客戶談話

MP3
07

英語會話到底什麼場合要用現在進行式？一個最基本的概念就是：
凡是說話時所提到的那件事與「說話的當時」有關，都用現在進行式。

你的中學英文法學得「很好」，現在還記得「感官動詞 hear（聽
見）、smell（聞到）、see（看見）等不要用進行式」的文法規則，你
現在可以把它從記憶中徹底清除，只要記得你說話時要表達的是「此
時此刻」就可以大大方方地用現在進行式。如：They are seeing
each other. 他們兩人正在交往。，即是一句很漂亮的純美語，說的
是男女之間的交往。

「句型練習」的例句應用在各種不同的場合，但表達的都是因為正
在做某件事，而無暇顧及另一件事，所以都用現在進行式來表達，注
意學習。

對話一

☺ M: Hold on.

請稍候，電話別掛斷。

I am talking with a client on the other line.

我正在另一條線上跟一個客戶談話。

☺ W: I just have a quick question.

我只要問一個很短的問題。

☺ M: Go ahead.

請說。

☺ W: I'm working on this report.

我正在做這份報告。

And I need your references.

而我需要你的參考資料。

☺ M: They are in my "work" directory on the "C" drive.

它們都在我的 C 硬碟裡面，在叫做「work」的目錄下。

對話二

☺ M: I am trying to put this in the simplest terms.

我試著盡量把這些用最簡單的話來說明。

☺ W: Well, I still do not understand.

嗯，我還是不明白。

☺ M: We are behind schedule on the China project.

那個「中國」的企劃案，我們的進度落後了。

☺ W: I got you there.

我懂了。

How do I fit in?

我該怎麼幫忙？

☺ M: I need two of your technicians to help with the mapping.

我需要你的兩個技術人員，來幫忙繪圖。

☺ W: O.K. Simple enough.

沒問題。那很簡單。

對話三

☺ M: Did you hear about John?

你聽到有關約翰的事嗎？

☺ W: Talk to me later, I'm thinking.

待會再跟我說，我現在在想事情。

☺ M: Sorry, didn't mean to interrupt.

對不起，我並不是故意要打斷你。

☺ W: It's okay.

沒關係。

I am just in the middle of some intense calculations.

我只是在做一些密集運算，剛好做到一半。

句型練習

1 Please be quiet. I am listening to the news report.

請安靜。我正在聽新聞報導。

2 I am writing my daily report, so I cannot talk now.

我正在寫我的每日報告,所以現在無法講話。

3 Can you hold this real quick, I am in the middle of carrying this package upstairs.

你可以稍微先幫我拿一下這個東西嗎,我正要帶這個包裹到樓上去。

4 I'm working right now, can I call you later?

我現在在工作,可以稍後再打電話給你嗎?

5 I am answering calls for John during lunch, so I can't go with you.

午餐時間我在替約翰接電話,所以不能跟你去。

基礎單字

✪ **client** [ˈklaɪənt]	客戶
✪ **line**	電話線
✪ **reference** [ˈrɛfərəns]	參考資料
✪ **drive**	硬碟
✪ **directory** [dəˈrɛktərɪ]	目錄

❂ **simplest** [ˈsɪmplɪst]	最簡單的
❂ **term**	詞彙；名詞
❂ **understand**	了解
❂ **schedule** [ˈskɛdʒʊl]	排定
❂ **technician** [tɛkˈnɪʃən]	技術人員
❂ **interrupt** [ˌɪntəˈrʌpt]	打斷談話
❂ **middle**	在～當中
❂ **intense** [ɪnˈtɛns]	密集的
❂ **calculation** [ˌkælkjəˈleʃən]	計算
❂ **news**	新聞
❂ **daily**	每日的
❂ **package** [ˈpækɪdʒ]	包裹
❂ **upstairs**	樓上

慣用語

❂ **on the other line**	在另一條電話線上
❂ **news report**	新聞報導
❂ **right now**	現在

Are you going to Taipei this weekend?

這個週末你要去台北嗎？

　　學校的英文測驗很喜歡考換字，be going to＝will 或 shall，表示「將要」，在學正確的英語會話時，你也可以把這個忘掉，別去理他什麼等於什麼，天底下的語言，每個字詞都有各自的含意，沒有百分之百相同的意思，講 be going to 就是 be going to，不用在去理會 will、shall。

　　be going to 指的是「即將」要做某件事沒錯，但記得，並不是僅有 going to 才表示「即將」，所有的動詞的進行式都可以指「即將」要做那個動作，例如：Are you coming tonight? 的 coming 不是說「正在來」，tonight 是「今晚」，時間都還沒到呢，怎能「正在來」。所以它的意思是 tonight 距離現在不久了，「你會來嗎？」

　　本課的重點就是用進行式來表示「馬上要做的事」。

對話一

☺ M: Are you going to Taipei this weekend?
　　 這個週末你要去台北嗎？

☺ W: Yes, I am attending a course on mapping.
　　 是的，我要去參加一個繪圖的課程。

☺ M: How long will you be gone?
　　 你要去多久？

☺ W: Two weeks.

兩個禮拜。

☺ M: Well, have fun.

那，祝你玩得愉快。

對話二

☺ M: Are you getting a new car soon?

你很快會買新車嗎？

☺ W: No, I decided to have my old one fixed.

不，我決定把我的舊車拿去修理。

☺ M: Why is that?

為什麼呢？

☺ W: Well, with the kids going off to school soon, we just couldn't afford it.

嗯，孩子們很快就要上學讀書，我們負擔不起。

對話三

☺ M: Are you playing football this season?

這一季你要打足球嗎？

☺ W: No, I hurt my knee.

不打，我的膝蓋受傷了。

☺ M: Really?
真的嗎？

I never knew.
我都不知道。

☺ W: Yeah, it got twisted in practice this summer.
是啊，今年夏天練習的時候扭傷了。

☺ M: I am sorry to hear that.
很難過聽到這件事。

☺ W: It is no big deal.
也沒什麼大不了。

I am going to try out for golf.
我要去參加高爾夫球的選拔。

句型練習

❶ Are you bringing the soft drinks tonight?
你今晚會帶冷飲來嗎？

❷ When are you leaving for China?
你什麼時候要離開前往中國？

❸ Are you working on the project next week?
下個禮拜你要作這個專劃嗎？

❹ Who is going to the conference?

誰要去參加研討會？

❺ I am planning to keep the trophy at home.

我打算把這個獎盃放在家裡。

基礎單字

☉ **attending** [əˈtɛndɪŋ]	參加	
☉ **course** [kors]	課程	
☉ **fixed**	修理好	
☉ **afford** [əˈfɔrd]	負擔得起	
☉ **season**	季	
☉ **twisted** [ˈtwɪstɪd]	扭傷	
☉ **practice**	練習	
☉ **conference** [ˈkɑnfərəns]	研討會	
☉ **trophy** [ˈtrofɪ]	獎盃	

慣用語

☉ **how long**	多久
☉ **next week**	下星期

8 Is John coming with us for lunch?

約翰要跟我們一道去吃午飯嗎？

MP3
09

如果你徹底瞭解上一課的會話，本課就很簡單。

現在進行式除了可以表示「即將」的動作、最近要做的事之外，還可以表示「預定」的事。

「句型練習」裡每一例句都是這種情形，例如：John is playing tennis on Monday 指的是約翰「已經決定」Monday 要 play tennis，不是正在 play tennis，這是最漂亮的美語。很多人説這句話時，可能想到「星期一」Monday 是未來的時間，脱口就説 John will play tennis on Monday.，注意：will 有表示一個人的意志性，用在表示未來的情況時，是很強烈的字眼，約翰雖然要打球，也未必有打不成球就成仁的決心吧？這就是為什麼英美人士多用 is playing tennis on Monday 的原因，而不説 will play tennis。

本書後面會學習到 will 的用法。

對話一

☺ M: Is John coming with us for lunch?

約翰要跟我們一起去吃午飯嗎？

☺ W: No, he is going later this afternoon.

不，下午晚一點他才會去。

☺ M: Why?

為什麼呢？

☺ W: We need someone to cover phones.

我們需要有人接電話。

☺ M: I sure hope they get a new receptionist soon.

我真希望他們很快雇一個新接待員。

對話二

☺ M: How is the family?

你府上家人都好嗎？

☺ W: Good.

很好。

My son is playing first chair violin tonight in the school orchestra.

我兒子在今天晚上的學校交響樂團上，將是第一小提琴手。

☺ M: Really?!

真的啊?!

That's fantastic!

那太棒了！

☺ W: Thanks.

謝謝你。

We are very excited.

我們都覺得很興奮。

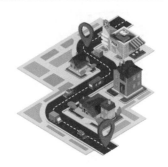

對話三

☺ M: John sure is busy working on that project.

約翰作那個企劃，真是忙。

☺ W: I know.

我知道。

I asked him to lunch yesterday, but he couldn't get away.

昨天我邀他一起去吃午飯，但是他走不開。

☺ M: No one is helping him get it done.

沒有人幫他做。

☺ W: Well, with Tom gone, we have been really shorthanded.

是啊，湯姆離職了，我們真是缺乏人手。

☺ M: Personnel will be hiring someone soon.

人事部很快就會再雇人的。

句型練習

❶ John is playing tennis on Monday with Tom.

約翰星期一要跟湯姆打網球。

❷ John is flying out next week to assess the situation.

約翰下個禮拜會搭飛機過去，評估情況。

❸ They are calling tomorrow for the production results.

他們明天會打電話來問製作結果。

❹ Mary is going to Paris Friday for the meeting.

瑪莉星期五要去巴黎開會。

❺ Peter is leaving Monday for his new job.

彼得星期一要離職，去做他的新工作。

基礎單字

✪ **orchestra** [ˈɔrkɪstrə]	弦樂隊
✪ **fantastic** [fænˈtæstɪk]	（口語）好極了
✪ **excited**	興奮的
✪ **shorthanded**	人手不夠
✪ **personnel**	人事部
✪ **receptionist** [rɪˈsɛpʃənɪst]	接待員
✪ **assess**	評估
✪ **situation**	情況
✪ **production** [prəˈdʌkʃən]	製作
✪ **result**	結果

慣用語

✪ **first chair**	首席
✪ **get away**	離開

9 I am going to go to the bookstore tonight.

今天晚上我要去書店

現在進行式在英語會話所佔的份量有越來越重的趨勢，越來越多人習慣用進行式，一定要學到能徹底應用才好。

對話一

☺ M: I am going to go to the bookstore tonight.

今天晚上我要去書店。

☺ W: What are you looking for?

你要買什麼？

☺ M: A book about Gardening.

一本有關於園藝的書。

☺ W: I didn't know you liked gardening.

我不知道你喜歡園藝。

☺ M: I am planning to take it up as a new hobby.

我打算培養園藝做我的新嗜好。

對話二

☺ M: What are your plans for the weekend?

這個週末你計劃做什麼？

☺ W: I hope to be going fishing.

我希望去釣魚。

☺ M: Where at?

去哪裡釣魚？

☺ W: I am driving north to the lake.

我打算開車到北邊的湖去。

☺ M: I have heard it is nice there.

我聽說那個地方很不錯。

對話三

☺ M: Are you going to watch the football game on TV tonight.

今晚你打算看電視上的足球賽嗎？

☺ W: No, I have to do paperwork at home.

不，我必需在家裡整理一些文件。

☺ M: What is the paperwork for?

那些文件是做什麼的？

☺ W: Our proposal for the new project.

我們對這個新專案的企劃。

☺ M: Good luck!

祝你一切順利！

句型練習

① There's a movie on TV tonight. Are you going to watch it?

今天晚上電視上有一部電影，你會看嗎？

② Are you planning to come in to work this weekend?

這個週末你要來上班嗎？

③ I am going to bring cookies to tomorrow's meeting.

明天的會議我會帶餅乾來。

④ We are all watching the game at John's house tonight.

今天晚上我們全部會聚在約翰家裡看比賽。

基礎單字

○ **hobby**	嗜好
○ **paperwork**	紙上作業
○ **cookie** [ˈkʊkɪ]	餅乾
○ **soccer** [ˈsɑkɚ]	足球
○ **company** [ˈkʌmpənɪ]	公司
○ **proposal**	企畫案

慣用語

○ **go fishing**	去釣魚

10 I was planning to fish this weekend, but~

這個週末我原本要去釣魚，但是～

現在進行式可以表示「預定」要做的事，那麼過去進行式就是表示過去本來定好要做的事。

本課的學習重點就是原本預定要做一件事，卻因某種原因沒有做成，例如：「我原本要看電影，但是來不及了沒看。」就是最典型的這種句型使用的時機，它的英語是 I was going to see a movie, but I was too late for it.

對話一

☺ M: I was planning to fish this weekend, but I had to work.

這個週末我原本要去釣魚，但是我必須上班。

☺ W: Really?

真的嗎？

☺ M: Yeah, our partners on the China project wanted their data today.

是啊，我們那件「中國」專案的合夥人，今天來要他們的資料。

☺ W: John couldn't do it?

這件事約翰不能做嗎？

☺ M: There was too much work for one person.
太多工作，一個人做不來。

☺ W: That was nice of you to help him out.
你人真好，能幫他做。

對話二

☺ M: We were going to visit you last night, but we thought it was too late.
昨天晚上我們本來要去拜訪你，但是我們覺得太晚了。

☺ W: What time was it?
那時候是幾點？

☺ M: About 9:00 p.m.
大約晚上九點。

☺ W: Actually it was best that you didn't.
事實上，你們沒來最好。

I was pretty tired.
我非常累。

☺ M: I am glad that we didn't then.
那我很慶幸我們沒去。

對話三

☺ M: John was planning to finish the poster last night.
昨天晚上約翰原本計劃要把海報做完。

But he had to take his wife to the doctor.

但是他必須帶他太太去看醫生。

☺ W: That's no problem.

不要緊。

We don't need it for another week.

我們一個禮拜之後才用得到它。

☺ M: I'll tell him.

我會告訴他。

He was pretty worried.

他非常擔心。

☺ W: I'll tell him.

我來告訴他。

☺ M: Thanks, Mary.

謝謝你，瑪莉。

Let me know if you need anything.

如果妳需要什麼的話，請告訴我。

句型練習

❶ I was going to pick up John, but I forgot.

我本來要去接約翰，但是我忘了。

❷ We were going to meet Friday, but Mary was out of town.

我們本來星期五要碰面，但是瑪莉到外地去了。

❸ He planned to call you, but had to go to an emergency meeting instead.

他本來要打電話給你，但是卻必須去參加一項緊急會議。

❹ I wanted to go to the movies last night, but I had too much to do.

昨天晚上我本來要去看電影，但是我有太多事情要做。

❺ I thought I would be able to call you last night, but I was busy.

我原本以為昨天晚上可以打電話給你，但是我很忙。

基礎單字

○ **fish**	釣魚
○ **partner** [ˈpɑrtnɚ]	合夥人
○ **data**	資料
○ **tired**	疲倦的
○ **poster** [ˈpostɚ]	海報
○ **worried**	擔憂的
○ **emergency** [ɪˈmɝdʒənsɪ]	緊急的
○ **busy**	忙碌的

慣用語

○ **go to the movies**	去看電影
○ **last night**	昨晚
○ **be able to**	能夠

第 3 章

用英語
請人幫忙秘訣
-WILL

11 I'll stay home this evening.

今天晚上我會待在家裡

既然最純正的英語會話，表示「即將的未來」可以用進行式，表示「預定好的未來」也可以用進行式，那麼文法書上說的未來式助動詞 will、shall 又是怎麼一回事？

與其要說 will、shall 表示「未來」，不如說是表示說話的人「要」做的事、或「決定會」做的事，例如：I'll say home. 講的是「我要待在家裡。」，有了這樣清楚的觀念你的英語就會突飛猛進了。

對話一

☺ M: Are you ready to go?

你準備好可以走了嗎？

☺ W: No, I'm too tired.

不，我太累了。

I think I'll stay home this evening.

我想我今天晚上要待在家裡。

☺ M: Come on.

走吧。

It will be fun!

會很好玩的！

☺ W: No, I have to be at work early tomorrow.

不行，我明天必須很早去上班。

☺ M: Suit yourself.

隨你便好了。

對話二

☺ M: Did you bring me that disk?

你有沒有帶磁碟片來給我？

☺ W: Oh, I forgot!

哦，我忘了！

☺ M: No problem, just bring it tomorrow.

沒有關係，明天帶來好了。

☺ W: I think I'll just go home at lunch and get it.

我想我還是在午飯的時候回家去拿。

☺ M: If it's not a problem, that would help me out a lot.

如果你可以的話，那可以幫我很大的忙。

對話三

☺ M: Where are you going?

你要去哪裡？

☺ W: I was going to grab a quick bite to eat.

我本來是要隨便去買個東西吃。

☺ M: Where are you planning to eat?

你打算到哪裡吃？

☺ W: I don't know!

我不知道！

I think I might go out for Greek food.

我想我可能去吃希臘食物。

☺ M: Sounds good. Mind if I join you?

聽起來很好。你介意我跟你一起去嗎？

☺ W: Not at all.

不介意。

句型練習

❶ I believe I'll have the steak with salad.

我想我要牛排沙拉。

❷ I think I'll ask Mary out to dinner.

我想我會邀瑪莉出去吃晚飯。

❸ I can't decide. I'll just have the house special.

我沒辦法做決定。我就要特餐好了。

④ I feel pretty bad. I think I'll call you back later.

我覺得很不舒服。我想我稍後再打電話給你。

⑤ I think I'll drive over to John's and pick up that report.

我想我會開車到約翰家，去拿那份報告。

基礎單字

✪ **disk**	磁碟
✪ **problem** [ˈprɑbləm]	問題
✪ **grab** [græb]	匆忙地拿
✪ **bite**	吃一口
✪ **mind**	介意
✪ **join**	加入
✪ **special** [ˈspɛʃəl]	特餐

慣用語

✪ **house special**	本店的特餐
✪ **stay home**	留在家
✪ **call you back**	再打電話給你
✪ **pick up something**	拿某樣東西
✪ **not at all**	一點也不
✪ **grab a bite**	隨便吃一點

12 I'll do that right away.

我立刻就去辦

will 具有表示「決定要做」的含意，即是「不打馬虎眼」，所以用在商務英語、服務業、下對上等時機最好，讓對方聽起來很受用，覺得很受尊重。

對話一

☺ M: What are you working on right now?
你現在在做什麼？

☺ W: The final report for the new project.
那一個新專案的最終報告。

☺ M: I need the financial summary for the quarter before lunch.
午餐以前我需要這一季的財務總結書。

☺ W: I'll do that right away.
我立刻去辦。

☺ M: Thanks.
謝謝你。

對話二

☺ M: Can you pick up a package for me?

你可以去幫我拿個包裹嗎？

☺ W: Where is it at?

在哪裡？

☺ M: The Federal Express distribution center.

「聯邦快遞」的分發中心。

☺ W: Sure.

好的。

I will drive over there and get it during lunch.

午餐時間我會開車過去拿。

對話三

☺ M: I'm sorry to have spilled coffee on your newspaper.

很抱歉我把咖啡濺在你的報紙上。

☺ W: Don't worry.

別擔心。

I won't hold it against you.

我不會記恨在心。

☺ M: I can go and buy you another.

我可以再去幫你買一份。

☺ W: Really, it is no big deal.

真的，那沒什麼大不了。

I had already read it.

我已經看過了。

☺ M: Okay, but I am still getting you one tomorrow morning.

好吧，但是明天早上我還是會幫你買一份。

句型練習

① We'll keep you informed of any changes to the agenda.

如果預定事項有任何改變的話，我們會隨時通知你。

② I'll get the ladder for you if you can't reach the light.

如果你夠不著那個電燈的話，我會拿梯子給你。

③ I won't let the dog out without his collar.

狗要是沒有戴頸圈，我不會讓牠出去。

④ John will keep the house clean while you are gone.

你們不在的時候，約翰會保持這個房子的清潔。

⑤ I'll call John right away and tell him about tonight.

我會馬上打電話給約翰，告訴他今晚的事。

基礎單字

○ **final**	最後的
○ **financial** [faɪˈnænʃəl]	財務的
○ **summary** [ˈsʌmərɪ]	總結
○ **quarter**	一季
○ **package**	包裹
○ **distribution** [ˌdɪstrəˈbjuʃən]	分發
○ **center**	中心
○ **spilled**	潑灑
○ **inform**	通知
○ **agenda** [əˈdʒɛndə]	預定事項
○ **reach**	達到
○ **ladder** [ˈlædɚ]	梯子
○ **collar** [ˈkɑlɚ]	領圈

慣用語

○ **right now**	現在
○ **Federal Express**	聯邦快遞

13 The car won't start.

車子發動不起來

MP3
14

本課來學 will 的最極端用法，也就是所謂的表示「意志」。

在做英語交談時，如果要表示「一定」、「無論如何也不能改變情況」的事，就用 will。例如本課的標題情況是「車子無論怎麼啟動，都發動不起來」，所以說 The car won't (will not) start.，講這句話已經含有說話的人試了又試，還是不起作用的挫折感，英語流利的人絕對會聽出這種挫折感的。學英語，一定要知道在學什麼，七情六慾都要能化為語言，傳達給對方，才叫流利，反過來說，對方話中有話，你還聽不出來，可就成了木頭了。

對話一

☺ M: The car won't start.

車子發動不起來。

☺ W: Did you check the battery connections?

你有沒有檢查電池接頭？

☺ M: No. I'll check them out.

沒有。我會查查看。

☺ W: If they are connected, turn on the headlights to see if they work.

如果電池有接好，把車頭燈打開，看是否會亮。

☺ M: Okay.

好的。

對話二

☺ M: I can't help you with your report.

我不能幫你做你的報告。

☺ W: Why not?

為什麼不行？

☺ M: It just would not be honest.

那是不誠實的行為。

☺ W: I don't want you to write it, just give me a little help.

我不要你替我寫，我只要你幫我一點忙。

☺ M: Tell me exactly what you want help with and I will offer suggestions.

告訴我你到底需要什麼協助，我會提供你一些建議。

☺ M: Mary will not come to the party if John is there.

如果約翰參加宴會的話，瑪莉不會去。

☺ W: She needs to be a little more mature.

她不要那麼孩子氣，應該要成熟一點。

☺ M: I think she is.

我認為她是成熟。

John will make a big scene and ruin the party.

約翰才是會小題大作，把整個宴會搞砸。

☺ W: That is nice of her to think about everyone else.

她能夠替其他人著想真好。

句型練習

❶ The dog will not come inside.

狗不會進來。

❷ Okay, I will help John write the report.

好的，我會幫約翰寫報告。

❸ I can't let you in without an invitation.

沒有邀請卡，我不能讓你進來。

❹ The computer won't let me do that.

電腦不允許我那麼做。

❺ John won't be coming to the meeting.

約翰不會來參加會議。

基礎單字

✪ **check**	檢查
✪ **battery** ['bætərɪ]	電池
✪ **connection** [kə'nɛkʃən]	接觸
✪ **headlight**	大燈
✪ **suggestion**	建議
✪ **exactly** [ɪg'zæktlɪ]	確切的
✪ **honest**	誠實的
✪ **mature** [mə'tʃʊr]	成熟
✪ **ruin**	破壞
✪ **invitation**	邀請卡
✪ **computer**	電腦

慣用語

✪ **turn on**	開燈
✪ **make a big scene**	小題大作；吵吵鬧鬧

14 I'll help you with the bag.

讓我來幫你提這個袋子

「要」幫別人忙，當然用 I'll 最好，表示自己的熱忱。

對話一

☺ M: The bag looks heavy.

這個袋子看起來很重。

I'll help you with it.

讓我來幫你提。

☺ W: Thanks. That's very nice of you.

謝謝你。你真好。

☺ M: It is really no problem.

真的沒有什麼關係。

☺ W: Well, it is rare these days for anyone to volunteer help.

嗯，近來已經很少人會自動幫助別人。

☺ M: I know.

我知道。

It is very sad.

那是很悲哀的事。

☺ M: How is your presentation coming?

你的簡報做得怎麼樣？

☺ W: Okay, but I am a little lost.

還好，但是我有一點失去頭緒。

☺ M: I'll be happy to help you with it.

我很樂意幫你忙。

☺ W: That would be great.

那好極了。

☺ M: What is giving you trouble?

哪一個部份有問題？

☺ W: The conclusion.

結尾的部份。

☺ M: I can work late if you need me to.

如果你有需要的話，我可以晚一點下班。

☺ W: Actually, that would be a big help.

事實上，那會很有幫助。

☺ M: Great. Let me just call home and let my wife know.

好。讓我打個電話回家，給我太太知道。

☺ W: If it's a problem, don't feel bad about going home.

如果有困難的話，你儘管回家沒有關係的。

☺ M: It is no problem at all.

一點困難都沒有。

I just don't want my wife to worry.

我只是不想讓我太太擔心而已。

句型練習

1 Why don't I help you move this weekend?

這個週末何不讓我來幫你搬家？

2 Let me get that door for you.

讓我來替你開門。

3 If you want, I'll keep minutes of the meeting.

如果你有需要的話，我可以替會議做記錄。

❹ That box looks full. Let me get another for you.

那個盒子看起來滿滿的。讓我替你另外拿一個。

❺ Let me get you a cup of coffee.

讓我替你倒一杯咖啡。

基礎單字

✪ **rare** [rɛr]	稀少
✪ **volunteer** [ˌvɑlənˈtɪr]	自願
✪ **minutes** [ˈmɪnɪts]	會議記錄
✪ **presentation**	簡報
✪ **conclusion** [kənˈkluʒən]	結尾
✪ **full**	滿的

慣用語

✪ **a cup of coffee**	一杯咖啡

15 Will you carry the bag for me?

你可以幫我拿這個袋子嗎？

請求別人幫忙，也是用 will 這個字，說 Will you…? 最好，表示「你有沒有決心」幫我忙，而不是「能不能」幫忙，讓對方連說 No 的勇氣都沒有，畢竟拒絕別人時說 I will not 我不幫要有很大的勇氣才說得出口。

對話一

☺ M: How is it going?

你好嗎？

☺ W: Pretty good, but I am having trouble with this map.

很好，但是這一張地圖實在是麻煩。

☺ M: What is the problem?

有什麼問題？

☺ W: It is too long.

它太長了。

Will you hold this end while I unroll it?

當我把它張開時，可否請你拿著這一端？

☺ M: No problem.

沒有問題。

對話二

☺ W: Did you just go to the store?

你剛去店裡買東西嗎？

☺ M: Yes, there are still several bags in the car.

是的，車子裡面還有好幾個袋子。

Would you mind helping me carry them in?

你介意幫我把它們拿進來嗎？

☺ W: Sure, where do you park your car?

可以的，你車子停在哪裡？

☺ M: Right next to your car.

就停在你車子旁邊。

☺ M: Will you find the November financial report for me, please?

你可以幫我找出十一月份的財務報告嗎？

☺ W: When do you need it by?

你什麼時候需要？

☺ M: Tomorrow morning.

明天早上。

☺ W: Great, I'll look for it after lunch.

好的，吃過午飯我就去找。

☺ M: Thank you.

謝謝你。

句型練習

❶ Will you carry that bag for me, please?

可否請你幫我拿那個袋子？

❷ Can you help John move that table into the other room?

你能夠幫約翰把那張桌子移到另外一個房間嗎？

❸ Would you mind helping me practice my English?

你介意協助我練習英文嗎？

❹ Do you think you could help me move this weekend?

你想這個週末你可以幫我搬家嗎？

❺ Could you please call the investors and give them a project update?

可否請你打電話給投資人，告訴他們這個案子最新的情況？

基礎單字

✪ **carry**	攜帶
✪ **unroll** [ʌn'rol]	展開
✪ **several**	好幾個
✪ **move**	搬家
✪ **investor** [ɪn'vɛstɚ]	投資者
✪ **update**	更新
✪ **park**	停車

慣用語

✪ **look for**	尋找
✪ **next to**	隔壁

16 When will you find out the results?

你什麼時候可以知道結果？

問別人幾時可以如何的英語，通常用 When will...? 的句型。

對話一

☺ M: How did your test go?

你的考試考得怎麼樣？

☺ W: I think I did pretty good.

我想我考得很好。

☺ M: When will you find out the results?

你什麼時候可以知道結果？

☺ W: I should hopefully find out by November.

十一月之前我應該可以知道。

☺ M: Let me know what you hear.

聽到什麼消息請讓我知道。

對話二

☺ M: I can't e-mail now.

我現在沒法寄電子郵件。

☺ W: What was the problem?

有什麼問題？

☺ M: Our network server went down last night.

我們的網路伺服器昨晚壞掉了？

☺ W: How will you know when you can mail again?

你怎麼知道什麼時候可以再寄？

☺ M: They'll call and leave a message.

他們會打電話來留話通知。

對話三

☺ M: Can you believe the weather?

你們相信天氣變化這麼大嗎？

☺ W: We'll probably be getting some rain tonight.

今天晚上可能會下雨噢。

☺ M: I guess so.

可能會。

☺ W: I had better bring my laundry in off the line before dark.

我最好在天黑前，把晾在繩子上的衣服收進來。

句型練習

❶ We'll hear from John in about a week.

大約一星期左右我們可以聽到約翰的消息。

② How long will you have to wait for that car?
為那一部車子你得等多久？

③ When will you be going on vacation?
你幾時要去度假？

④ I'll be getting my license soon.
我很快就會拿到我的執照。

⑤ John will be happy to see us.
約翰會很高興看到我們。

基礎單字

✪ **test**		測驗
✪ **hopefully**		希望
✪ **network**		網路
✪ **server** [ˈsɝvɚ]		伺服器
✪ **message** [ˈmɛsɪdʒ]		留話
✪ **weather**		氣候
✪ **laundry** [ˈlɔndrɪ]		洗好的衣服
✪ **line**		晾衣線
✪ **license** [ˈlaɪsəns]		執照

慣用語

✪ **find out**	知道
✪ **at least**	至少
✪ **before dark**	天黑之前
✪ **wait for**	等候
✪ **go on vacation**	度假

17 I'll call you when I get there.

我到了那裡會打電話給你

will 既然能表示「意志」，就可以用來表示「承諾」。I'll do it. 的話已經含有「我承諾我一定會做」的的意思，在英語會話中，這種用法已經普遍到有時說話的人都忘了「承諾」是要負責任的，變成僅是口頭語了。

對話一

☺ M: Have a good flight!

祝你一路順風！

☺ W: Thanks.

謝謝你。

I'll call you when I get there.

我到了那裡會打電話給你。

☺ M: Sounds good.

很好。

Be sure to get rested first though.

不過你還是要先好好休息。

☺ W: I will.

我會的。

I am sure the jet lag will keep me tired.

我相信時差一定會使我覺得很累。

對話二

☺ M: Can John come over tonight?

約翰今天晚上會過來嗎？

☺ W: He said he would come over when the baby-sitter shows up.

他說等褓母到的時候，他就來。

☺ M: When will that be?

那要到什麼時候？

☺ W: He didn't know.

他不知道。

The baby-sitter has to pick her younger brother up from soccer practice first.

褓母得先去足球練習場接她弟弟。

☺ M: Well, I guess I'll put dinner in the oven to keep it warm.

那我想我還是把晚餐放在烤爐保溫。

☺ M: Do you have the report ready yet?

你的報告做好了嗎？

☺ W: No.

還沒有。

I'll bring it to you when I finish with the editing.

等我編輯好，我就會拿給你。

☺ M: Okay.

好。

I just wanted to see how it was coming.

我只是想知道報告做得怎麼樣了。

☺ W: It is about ninety percent done.

大約完成了九〇%。

句型練習

❶ I'll stop by when I get a chance.

有空我會過來坐坐。

❷ I will be sure to let you know when I am ready to print the document.

當我準備好要印文件的時候，一定會讓你知道。

第 3 章 用英語請人幫忙秘訣 WILL

81

❸ We'll be able to leave when the repairman is done.

等修理員修好之後，我們就可以離開。

❹ I can come over when I am finished with my homework.

等我把家庭作業作完，我就可以到你家來。

基礎單字

✪ **flight** [flaɪt]	班機
✪ **baby-sitter**	褓母
✪ **oven**	火爐
✪ **editing**	編輯
✪ **percent** [pɚˋsɛnt]	百分比
✪ **document** [ˋdɑkjəˌmɛnt]	文件
✪ **homework**	家庭作業
✪ **repairman**	修理工人

慣用語

✪ **get rested**	休息
✪ **jet lag**	時差
✪ **show up**	出現；到達
✪ **get home**	回到家

18 I'll let you know.

我會通知你

will 表示「承諾」經常與其他的詞連用，以加強語氣，表示該承諾在一定的時間保證會兌現。once（一旦）、 as soon as（一旦…馬上）等都是這種連用的詞。

對話一

☺ M: Is the presentation ready yet?
　　簡報準備好了嗎？

☺ W: Not quite.
　　還沒完全好。

　　I'll let you know as soon as I finish it.
　　我一完成，就通知你。

☺ M: Good.
　　好的。

　　We are anxious to see it.
　　我們急著想看看。

☺ W: I am anxious to have it done, too!
　　我也很急著想把它做完！

☺ M: When will you know this weekend?

這個週末你什麼時候可以知道？

☺ W: I am waiting on the boss.

我在等我老闆做決定。

☺ M: We are trying to make travel arrangements.

我們正想辦法要做旅行安排呢。

☺ W: I know.

我知道。

I will let you know as soon as I can.

我會盡可能早點通知你。

☺ M: Okay, thanks.

好的，謝謝。

對話三

☺ M: Have you heard who won the race?

你有沒有聽說誰贏得選戰？

☺ W: No.

沒有。

I'll let you know as soon as I find out.

我一知道就告訴你。

☺ M: I will do the same.

我也一樣。

☺ W: Sounds good.

很好。

I'll talk to you later then.

那我以後再跟你聊。

句型練習

❶ As soon as I know who is going, I'll give you a call.

等我一知道誰要去，我就給你打電話。

❷ I will write you as soon as I get settled in to my new home.

等我把我新家安頓好，我就會寫信給你。

❸ John will let you know as soon as he gets done with the project.

約翰一把他的案子做完，就會通知你。

❹ The car will be sold as soon as John comes back with his money.

等約翰拿錢來，這部車子就可以賣掉。

⑤ I will paint the house as soon as I can.

我會盡快油漆這棟房子。

基礎單字

✪ **finish**		完成
✪ **anxious** [ˈæŋkʃəs]		渴望的；急切的
✪ **boss**		老闆
✪ **arrangement** [əˈrendʒmənt]		安排
✪ **race**		比賽
✪ **paint**		油漆

慣用語

✪ **wait on**	等候決定

19 You'll get wet.

你會淋濕的

will 因為具有強烈的語氣，所以也可以拿來做警告之用，表示不聽忠告，就「必定」會有不良的後果。

對話一

☺ M: I am going to go for a walk.

我要出去散步。

☺ W: It's raining.

正在下雨呢。

You'll get wet if you go out.

如果你出去，你會淋濕的。

☺ M: A little rain never hurt anyone.

一點點雨傷不了任何人的。

☺ W: No, but it is also cold.

是不會，但是外面也很冷。

☺ M: Well, maybe I had better stay in then.

嗯，那麼或許我最好還是留在屋裡。

☺ M: Did you watch the debate last night?

你有沒有看昨天晚上的辯論？

☺ W: No. I'll get sick if I have to listen to anymore political discussion.

沒有。如果我還得再聽任何政治討論，我一定會生病。

☺ M: How will you know who to vote?

你怎能知道你要投給誰？

☺ W: I just go by what I read in the papers.

看報紙怎麼說，我就投給誰。

☺ M: Do what you like, but I like to form my own opinions.

隨便你，但我喜歡有我自己的意見。

☺ M: I will keep your dog for you if you supply the food.

如果你供應食物的話，我可以幫你看你的狗。

☺ W: That sounds great.

主意不錯噢！。

☺ M: Good.

好。

I know how it is when you have to travel.

我可以體會一個人必須出差時，會是什麼情況。

☺ W: Yeah.

是啊。

It is hard to keep pets with a job like this.

有這樣一個工作，實在很難養寵物。

☺ M: I used to have to do it, too.

我從前也必須出差的。

句型練習

❶ John will mow the grass while we are gone if we leave him the key to the garage.

當我們不在的時候，如果我們把到車庫的鑰匙留給約翰，他會幫我們割草。

❷ I'll go to the store if you tell me what to get.

如果你告訴我要買什麼，我可以到店裡去買。

❸ You'll catch a cold if you go out without a jacket.

如果你出門不穿夾克的話，你會著涼的。

❹ The battery will die if you leave the lights on.

如果你讓燈開著的話，電池會沒有電。

❺ The car will stall if you don't give it some gas.

如果你不加點油的話，車子會熄火。

☼	**hurt**	傷害
☼	**political** [pə'lɪtɪk!]	政治的
☼	**discussion**	討論
☼	**debate**	辯論
☼	**paper**	報紙
☼	**supply** [sə'plaɪ]	供應
☼	**travel**	旅行
☼	**pet**	寵物
☼	**garage**	車庫
☼	**mow**	除草
☼	**jacket**	夾克
☼	**stall** [stɔl]	汽車等的拋錨

慣用語

☼	**go for a walk**	散步
☼	**get wet**	淋濕
☼	**had better**	最好
☼	**catch a cold**	感冒

20 John will be taking calls while we go to lunch.

我們吃午餐的時候，約翰會接電話

英語會話中表示「當什麼情況發生時」，最常用的英文字有 when 和 while，一般亞洲人士比較不會用 while，所以本課就來學這個字的用法。

對話一

☺ M: John will be taking calls while we go to lunch.

我們去吃午飯的時間，約翰會接電話。

☺ W: How did he end up with that job?

怎麼會由他來做這個工作呢？

☺ M: He was late to work this morning.

今天早上他上班遲到。

☺ W: That seems a little harsh.

那似乎也很太嚴厲。

☺ M: Not really, it was his third day in a row.

也不盡然，他已經一連三天都遲到了。

對話二

☺ M: Can you take care of the plants while I'm on vacation?

我去度假的時候，你可以幫我照顧花草嗎？

☺ W: I can for a while, but I am going to be out of the office, too.

我可以做一陣子，但是我自己也要去出差。

☺ M: I might ask John then.

那麼我可能會請約翰來做。

☺ W: That's probably a good idea.

可能那樣做比較好。

對話三

☺ M: Will you go sightseeing while you are in New York?

你到紐約的時候，會去觀光嗎？

☺ W: No. The meeting schedule is very tight.

不。會議的行程非常緊湊。

☺ M: I heard you would only be gone two days.

我聽說你只去兩天。

☺ W: Yes, but I am taking a third day off to recover from the jet lag.

是的，但是第三天我請假，好恢復時差。

☺ M: Good idea.

好主意。

句型練習

❶ I will hold calls while you are in the meeting.

你開會的時候，我不會把電話轉接過去給你。

❷ John can't work while you keep talking to him.

你一直跟約翰講話，他無法工作。

❸ I can't drink alcohol while I am on this medication.

我作這種藥物治療的時候，不可以喝酒。

❹ Would you answer my phone while I run down the hall?

我去走廊那邊一下，你可否幫我接電話？

❺ Can you check my spelling while I call Mary?

當我打電話給瑪莉時，你可否幫我檢查拼字？

基礎單字

✪ **harsh** [hɑrʃ]		嚴厲的
✪ **tight** [taɪt]		緊的
✪ **plant**		植物
✪ **probably**		可能
✪ **recover** [rɪˈkʌvɚ]		恢復
✪ **medication** [ˌmɛdɪˈkeʃən]		藥物治療
✪ **alcohol**		酒
✪ **hall**		大廳
✪ **spelling**		拼字

慣用語

✪ **take care of**	照料
✪ **take call**	接電話
✪ **in a row**	接連

第 4 章

如何正確
表達事件的時間

21 Before you leave, you need to call John.

你離開之前要打電話給約翰

before 這個字除了表示位子的前後，例如 before you... （在你前面），也可以表示時間的前後，使用 before 要注意既然時間有前後，動作就有前後之分，所以動作的時態就很重要，英語對於動作的前後是很在意的，誤用時態會產生時間錯亂，這點要注意。

對話一

☺ M: Before you leave, you need to call John.
你離開之前，要打電話給約翰。

☺ W: What about?
有什麼事嗎？

☺ M: He didn't say.
他沒有說。

☺ W: I had better call then.

那麼我最好還是打給他。

☺ M: If he had said what he wanted, would you call him back?

如果他說了他要什麼，你還會打電話給他嗎？

☺ W: Not if it was something trivial.

如果是芝麻蒜皮的小事，我就不會打。

對話二

☺ M: I'll call you later tonight.

今天晚上稍晚我會打電話給你。

☺ W: Before you call me, see if you can get that hotel's phone number in New York.

你在打電話給我之前，看看能否找到紐約那家旅館的電話號碼。

☺ M: I thought you already had a room.

我以為你已經訂好房間了。

☺ W: The hotel was full.

旅館都客滿了。

☺ M: Before John is allowed to drive, he must first pass a test.

約翰可以開車之前，必須先通過一個測驗。

☺ W: What kind of test?

什麼樣的測驗？

☺ M: A driving test, and a written test over the traffic laws.

開車的路考以及有關交通規則的筆試。

☺ W: Is it hard?

很難嗎？

☺ M: Well, millions of others pass it every year.

這樣說吧，每年有幾百萬人考過。

☺ W: Good point.

說得好。

句型練習

❶ Before I go to the store, I need a list of what you want.

我到店裡購物之前，我要你列一張你要的東西。

❷ Before John can come over, you need to clean your room.

你必須先整理你的房間，約翰才可以過來。

❸ Before giving a presentation, you need to introduce yourself.

在你做簡報之前，必須先自我介紹。

❹ Before I write mom a letter, I need to call grandpa.

在我給媽媽寫信之前，我必須先打電話給祖父。

基礎單字

☺ **trivial** [ˈtrɪvɪəl]	不重要的
☺ **full**	客滿
☺ **traffic**	交通
☺ **law**	法律
☺ **million** [ˈmɪljən]	一百萬
☺ **pass**	通過
☺ **clean**	清理
☺ **introduce** [ˌɪntrəˈdjus]	介紹
☺ **point**	重點

慣用語

☺ **come over**	過來拜訪
☺ **call him back**	回他的電話

22 Wait here until I come back.

在這裡等我回來

表示事情發生的時間的英文字,最容易讓亞洲人士誤譯、誤用的是 until,它的意思是「直到」某件事發生時,「才可」做另一件事,但是 純正英語的表達法是用反面 not ~ until 來表達的,也就是說「直到」 某件事發生「之前」,「不可以」做另一件事,這種習慣上的不同, 造成學習的困擾,注意「句型練習」第 1、2、3 句的說法。

對話一

☺ M: Wait here until I come back.

在這裡等我回來。

☺ W: Where are you going?

你要去哪裡?

☺ M: I am just running across the street to get a candy bar.

我只是到對街去買個糖果。

☺ W: Okay. See you in a minute.

好的。等一下見。

對話二

☺ M: I can't wait until the Olympics start.
我等不及奧林匹克運動會開始。

☺ W: I also am excited.
我也是很興奮。

☺ M: What is your favorite event?
你最喜歡的項目是什麼？

☺ W: I like platform diving best.
我最喜歡高台跳水。

☺ M: I really like the cycling.
我實在很喜歡自行車比賽。

對話三

☺ M: Are you going home?
你要回家了嗎？

☺ W: No. I have to wait until this customer calls back.
沒有。我必須等到這個客人打電話回來。

☺ M: What is the call about?
打電話為什麼事？

☺ W: Their network went down this afternoon.

他們的網路今天下午當機了。

And they think it is our software.

而他們認為是我們的軟體引起的。

☺ M: Do you need any help?

你需要協助嗎？

☺ W: No, there is really nothing you can do.

不需要，你真的幫不上忙的。

句型練習

❶ John won't call until he gets to Paris.

約翰到巴黎之後才會打電話來。

❷ I will not be able to leave the house until the baby-sitter gets here.

褓母到了之後，我才可以離開家。

❸ You can have the trophy until we get a display case at the office.

你可以把獎盃留著，直到我們辦公室買展示櫃。

❹ Don't release the files until I check with the legal department.

在我跟法律部門查過之前，不要把檔案公開。

5 I have to wait until January to get a new computer.

我必須等到一月才可以買一個新的電腦。

基礎單字

☺ **candy**	糖果
☺ **favorite**	最喜歡的
☺ **cycling** [ˈsaɪklɪŋ]	自行車比賽
☺ **customer**	顧客
☺ **display** [dɪsˈple]	展示
☺ **case**	櫃子
☺ **legal** [ˈligl̩]	合法的
☺ **release**	公開
☺ **file**	檔案

慣用語

☺ **platform diving**	高台跳水
☺ **legal department**	法律部門
☺ **get to**	到達

23 After I'm done reading the book, you can borrow it.

MP3 24

我把這本書看完之後，可以借你

　　after 好像是很平常的一個字，但亞洲人說英語時，用這個字的句型，一般都不很純正。其實它的用法不難，after 的句子通常分成兩部分，和 before 的句型相同，指「做完某件事之後」，才做另一件事，那麼，after 所引導的動作「已經」做完了，所以可以用完成式「have+ 過去分詞」的格式，「be+ 過去分詞的格式」來表達就對了。

　　「句型練習」中的例句全部是用 have+ 過去分詞，學習時注意每一句的說法，同時注意時間前後關係，照著用就對了。。

對話一

☺ M: After I've done my math assignment, you can borrow the book.

　　當我把數學作業作好之後，你可以借這本書。

☺ W: How much more do you have to go?

你還有多少要做？

☺ M: I am about halfway done.

我差不多已經做了一半。

☺ W: I look forward to reading it.

我期待著看這本書。

☺ M: It really is very good.

這本書真的很好。

對話二

☺ M: How is it going?

你好嗎？

☺ W: Well, once I've finished this assignment, things will be a lot better.

嗯，只要我把這個分配到的工作做完，局面就會好很多。

☺ M: I know how you feel.

我知道你的感覺。

☺ W: Really?

真的？

☺ M: Yes, I had to complete the whole project by myself.

是的，我也曾必須獨自一個人把整個案子做完。

☺ M: After we finish this presentation, we should go out to celebrate.

等我們把簡報做完之後，應該出去慶祝一下。

☺ W: I think we should celebrate after we get the contract.

我認為我們應該拿到合約之後才慶祝。

☺ M: Do you think we won't get it?

你認為我們拿不到嗎？

☺ W: I am just saying that giving the presentation does not guarantee that we will get the contract.

我只是說，做了簡報並不保證我們一定可以拿得到合約。

句型練習

❶ After you have finished painting, you can wash the car.

你油漆完了之後，可以去洗車。

❷ After I've completed this report, I am going to take a day off.

當我把這篇報告做完之後，我要請一天假。

❸ Once I've finished working, I am going out

for a drink.

當我把工作做完之後，我要出去喝杯酒。

❹ After you've written your paper, you can help John with his.

你把報告寫完之後，可以幫約翰做他的。

❺ After I've written this article, you can have the computer.

等我把這篇文章寫完，你就可以用這台電腦。

基礎單字

✪ **assignment** [ə'saɪnmənt]	作業
✪ **halfway**	一半
✪ **complete**	完成
✪ **celebrate** ['sɛlə͵bret]	慶祝
✪ **contract** ['kɑntrækt]	合約
✪ **guarantee** [͵gærən'ti]	保證
✪ **article**	文章

慣用語

✪ **look forward to**	期待
✪ **take a day off**	請一天假

24 Where shall we go on vacation this summer?

今年夏天我們要去哪裡度假？

MP3 25

講英語時，要表示「應該」，就馬上想到要用 should 或 shall。不要把 shall 當未來式看待，以「應該」意思來思考，學習起來比較容易，說起話來也比較流利。

對話一

☺ M: Where shall we go on vacation this summer?

今年夏天我們要到什麼地方去度假？

☺ W: Let's go to Florida.

我們到佛羅里達去。

☺ M: Why Florida?

為什麼要去佛羅里達？

☺ W: I have always wanted to see the white sand beaches.

我一直想要去看看白色沙灘。

☺ M: I would like to do some diving, too.

我也想要去跳水。

對話二

☺ M: Where should I go to get a good deal on furniture?

我到哪裡可以買到物美價廉的家具？

☺ W: I like ABC's quite a bit.

我蠻喜歡 ABC 公司的。

☺ M: Where is the showroom at?

他們的展示室在哪裡？

☺ W: It is over on the West side of town.

在西區那一頭。

對話三

☺ M: Where should I look to find a good vet?

我要到哪裡找一個好的獸醫？

☺ W: Did you look in the phone book?

你有沒有找電話號碼簿？

☺ M: Yes, but there are hundreds listed.

有，但是上面列有好幾百個。

☺ W: I can ask my brother where he takes his pets.

我可以問我哥哥，看他都把寵物帶去哪裡。

☺ M: That would be great.

那很好。

❶ What should I do about John's plants?
約翰的花草我該怎麼辦？

❷ When should I apply for citizenship?
我何時該申請公民權？

❸ Where shall we go for dinner?
我們該去哪裡吃晚餐？

❹ Where shall we stay in Hong Kong?
到香港我們要住哪裡？

基礎單字

❂ **deal**	交易
❂ **furniture** [ˈfɝnɪtʃɚ]	家具
❂ **showroom**	展示室
❂ **beaches**	海邊
❂ **diving**	跳水
❂ **vet** [vɛt]	獸醫
❂ **citizenship** [ˈsɪtɪznʃɪp]	公民

慣用語

❂ **apply for**	申請

25 I phoned you last night.

昨天晚上我打電話給你

英語會話上使用過去式，最普通有兩個情況：一個很明顯有表示過去的時間，例如 last night 昨晚、last year 去年、yesterday 昨天等；另一種情形是交談的雙方都知道所說的是過去的某件事，不需要在特別指明時間，例如每星期一早上，各公司員工見面最常問好的話是 How was your weekend? 週末愉快嗎？，這裡雖然沒有特指時間的字眼，但絕對知道指的是剛過的週末，所以用過去式 was。

對話一

☺ M: I phoned you last night, but you weren't home.

昨天晚上我打電話給你，但是你不在家。

☺ W: I was out with my sister.

我跟我妹妹出去。

☺ M: Where did you go?

你們去哪裡？

☺ W: We went shopping for my mother's birthday present.

我們出去買給我母親的生日禮物。

☺ M: Sounds like fun.

那一定挺有意思囉。

對話二

☺ M: I tried to call you yesterday.

昨天我試著打電話給你。

☺ W: I wasn't home.

我不在家。

I had to go to Taipei for a meeting.

我到台北去開會。

☺ M: Why all the way to Taipei?

為什麼遠到台北去？

☺ W: Our investors from Hong Kong did not want to come to Tainan.

我們從香港來的投資人不要到台南來。

☺ M: The things we do for business!

做生意就是這樣！

對話三

☺ M: I tried to get John to come with us for lunch, but he wasn't at his desk.

我想要找約翰跟我們一起去吃午飯，但是他不在他的辦公室。

☺ W: I think he was having lunch with Mary.

我想他跟瑪莉去吃午飯。

☺ M: Are they dating?

他們兩個在約會嗎？

☺ W: I don't know.

我不清楚。

You will have to ask John.

你必須去問約翰。

句型練習

❶ I thought you were going to be home last night.

我以為你昨晚會在家。

❷ Was I supposed to call you this morning?

今天早上我是否該打電話給你？

❸ Were you out at the mall last night?

昨天晚上你到購物中心去逛街嗎？

④ I wasn't home last night.

昨天晚上我不在家。

⑤ We weren't able to go out last night.

昨天晚上我們沒辦法出去。

基礎單字

○ **phone**	打電話
○ **present** ['prɛzn̩t]	禮物
○ **meeting**	會議
○ **business**	生意

慣用語

○ **last night**	昨晚
○ **went shopping**	上街購物

26 I called you last night.

昨天晚上我打電話給你

MP3 27

為了讓對方知道某件事情已經發生，就用過去式，I called you. 指我「打過」電話了，而 I call you. 卻是無意義的話，若是說話的當時正好在打電話或是即將要打電話，則用現在進行式，說 I am calling you.。

對話一

☺ M: I called you last night.

昨天晚上我打電話給你。

☺ W: Yes. Mary gave me the message.

我知道。瑪莉給了我你的留言。

☺ M: It was not important.

也沒有什麼重要的事。

☺ W: I would have called back, but it was too late.

我本來要給你回電話，但是太晚了。

☺ M: I had a good time at the baseball game last night.

昨天晚上的棒球賽，我們玩得很起勁。

☺ W: Who all went?

有哪些人去？

☺ M: John, Mary and myself.

約翰、瑪莉，還有我。

☺ W: Did you have good seats?

你們買到好的座位嗎？

☺ M: Actually, we had very good seats.

事實上，我們的座位非常好。

對話三

☺ M: How was the trip?

你們的旅行玩得怎麼樣？

☺ W: We had a good vacation.

我們玩得非常愉快。

☺ M: You will have to tell me about it sometime.

你有空可得說給我聽。

☺ W: I will when I get the pictures developed.

我會的，等我把相片洗出來。

句型練習

① How was your trip?

你們的旅行玩得怎麼樣？

② We had a big meal.

我們吃得很豐盛。

③ She had a cold.

她感冒了。

④ I had three phone calls in an hour.

一個小時之內我接到三通電話。

⑤ I had a sandwich and a coke at my desk.

我桌上有三明治和一杯可樂。

基礎單字

○ **trip**	旅遊
○ **picture**	照片
○ **develop** [dɪˈvɛləp]	沖洗相片
○ **seats**	座位
○ **important**	重要的

慣用語

○ **in an hour**	一小時之內
○ **get the pictures developed**	把相片沖洗出來

27 I didn't do much work this morning.

今天早上我沒做多少事

MP3 28

在英語會話上,意義最清晰的是過去式的說法,除了指已經發生的事之外,沒有別的含意。但是對中國人來說,卻是最麻煩的事,因為中國語言動詞沒有過去式的變化,很多人沒有將英語動詞以過去式表達的習慣,結果會講出一些自以為對,歐美人卻聽不懂的話,如上課所舉的 I call you. 這種不知所云的句子。所以學過去式說法,首要就是要熟記每個動詞的過去式,其他按照本書給你的觀念來學就簡單了。

對話一

☺ **M:** How are things going?

事實進行得如何了?

☺ **W:** Okay.

還好。

I didn't do much work this morning.

今天早上我沒做多少事。

☺ M: Why not?

為什麼沒有？

☺ W: Mary kept interrupting me to help her write her report.

瑪莉三番兩次打斷我，要我幫她寫她的報告。

☺ M: Send her to me next time.

下一次叫她來找我。

對話二

☺ M: We didn't get to see the movie last night.

昨天晚上我們沒看得成電影。

☺ W: Why not?

為什麼呢？

☺ M: One of our kids got sick.

我們有一個小孩病了。

☺ W: I am sorry to hear that.

很遺憾聽到這樣的事。

☺ M: You didn't finish your work yesterday.

你昨天沒把工作做完。

☺ W: I know.

我知道。

I left you a phone message.

我打過電話，留了話給你。

☺ M: I got it, but I couldn't understand it.

我收到了，但是我聽不明白。

☺ W: My husband got in a car accident.

我先生出車禍。

And I went to the hospital to see him.

所以我到醫院去看他。

☺ M: I hope he is doing okay.

我希望他沒有大礙。

☺ W: Yes. He was not hurt badly.

還好。他沒有傷得很嚴重。

句型練習

❶ I wasn't able to finish my work.

我沒辦法完成我的工作。

② He wasn't around yesterday.

他昨天不在。

③ She didn't find him yesterday.

昨天她沒有找到他。

④ We didn't get much done last week.

上個禮拜我們沒有完成多少。

⑤ I couldn't find the store last night.

昨天晚上我們找不到那家店。

基礎單字

☺ **report**	報告
☺ **left**	留下（**leave** 的過去式）
☺ **accident** ['æksɪdənt]	意外事件
☺ **hospital** ['hɑspɪtl]	醫院
☺ **badly**	嚴重地

慣用語

☺ **car accident**	車禍
☺ **next time**	下一次
☺ **got sick**	病了

28 Did you enjoy the party?

宴會上你玩得愉快嗎?

MP3 29

對話一

☺ M: Did you enjoy the party last night?
昨天晚上,宴會上你玩得愉快嗎?

☺ W: Yes. It was a lot of fun.
是的。很好玩。

☺ M: I thought it was well put together.
我認為宴會辦得很好。

☺ W: It really was well organized.
的確是樣樣都組織得很好。

☺ M: I hope we do another next year.
我希望明年我們再辦一個。

對話二

☺ M: Did you watch the Olympics last night?
昨天晚上你有沒有看奧林匹克比賽?

☺ W: Yes. Wasn't it amazing?

看了。奧林匹克比賽真是嘆為觀止，不是嗎？

☺ M: I thought so, but my kids were not interested.

我是這麼想，但是我小孩不太感興趣。

☺ W: I wonder why.

我不懂為什麼？。

☺ M: They like the basketball, but not much else.

他們喜歡藍球，其它的就不太喜歡。

對話三

☺ M: We went to the baseball game last night.

昨天晚上我們去看棒球比賽。

☺ W: Have you been to the stadium before?

你們以前有沒有去過體育場？

☺ M: No. Last night was the first time.

沒有。昨天晚上是第一次。

☺ W: What did you think of it?

你認為怎麼樣？

☺ M: It was really nice.

非常好。

① Did you get some sleep last night?

昨天晚上你有沒有睡覺？

② Were you able to watch the game yesterday?

昨天你去看比賽了沒有？

③ Did you have a good vacation?

你們假期玩得愉快嗎？

④ Had you been to New York before?

你以前有沒有去過紐約？

⑤ Were you home last night?

昨天晚上你在家嗎？

基礎單字

✪ **enjoy**	喜歡
✪ **party**	宴會
✪ **fun**	樂趣
✪ **organized** [ˈɔrgənˌaɪzd]	有組織的；有條理的
✪ **amazing** [əˈmezɪŋ]	令人驚奇的
✪ **stadium** [ˈstedɪəm]	體育場

慣用語

✪ **next year**	明年
✪ **a lot of fun**	很有趣

第 5 章

完成式
在會話的應用

29 Have you traveled a lot?

你常常旅行嗎？

若是有一件事，確定已經發生，但沒有指明、也不需強調發生的特定時間，不可用過去式，要用現在完成式「have+ 過去分詞」的形式。例如 I ate an apple.（我吃蘋果了），ate 是過去式，這句話主要的重點在講「吃了」，而 I have eaten apples. 我曾經吃過蘋果，主要的重點在說「曾經」吃過，至於幾時吃的，並不重要。

上面這個觀念很重要，不要被「完成」式的「完成」二字侷限你說話時的思考。

對話一

☺ W: Have you traveled a lot, John?

約翰，你常常旅行嗎？

☺ M: Yes. Quite a bit.

是的。常常旅行。

☺ W: Where have you gone?

你去過什麼地方？

☺ M: Mostly South American countries.

大部份是南美的國家。

But I have been to Europe as well.

但是我也去過歐洲。

☺ W: I hope to travel someday, too.

我希望有一天我也去旅行。

對話二

☺ M: I've been out the last two weeks for training.

前兩個禮拜我都到外地去受訓。

☺ W: Where did you go?

你去哪裡？

☺ M: I went to Los Angeles.

我去洛杉磯。

☺ W: What did you work on?

你到那裡主要是做什麼？

☺ M: I worked on the new software testing.

我做新的軟體測試。

對話三

☺ M: We've gone to several companies with this offer.

我們拿著這個提案已經到過好幾家公司。

☺ W: What do they think?

他們認為怎麼樣？

☺ M: No one wants to invest in a risky case.

沒有人要投資在有風險的案子。

☺ W: Well, you cannot steal second base without taking your foot off of first.

嗯，一個人的腳不搶先離開一壘的話，就不可能成功地盜上二壘。

☺ M: I know. It's their loss.

我知道。所以那是他們的損失。

句型練習

❶ I've done the best I can.

我已經盡我可能的做了。

❷ We've given it a thorough evaluation.

我們已經針對它做了全盤的評估。

❸ You've been late three days in a row.

你已經連續三天遲到。

❹ I've been home the past few days.

過去幾天我都一直在家。

❺ I've spent too much time on this project.

在這個專案上我已經花了太多時間。

基礎單字

○ **training**	訓練
○ **offer** [ˈɔfɚ]	提案
○ **invest**	投資
○ **risky**	有風險的
○ **loss**	損失
○ **thorough** [ˈθɝo]	徹底的
○ **evaluation** [ɪˌvæljʊˈeʃən]	評估

慣用語

○ **as well**	也

30 Have you ever been to France?

你到過法國嗎？

Have you ever been to ~?或 I have been to ~.的句型都是完成式，所以表示「曾經」去過某個地方，重點是表示某種曾經發生的經驗。

對話一

☺ M: Have you ever been to France?

你到過法國嗎？

☺ W: Yes. I went in 1987 for vacation.

是的。一九八七年我去那裡度假。

☺ M: I really like it there.

我真的很喜歡那裡。

☺ W: It is nice.

那裡是很好。

Did you go for the company?

是公司派你去的嗎？

☺ M: Yes, we are closing the office over there.

是的，我們要關閉那邊的辦公室。

對話二

☺ M: Where are you going for vacation?

你要去哪裡度假？

☺ W: The Hawaiian Islands.

夏威夷群島。

Have you ever been there?

你去過那裡嗎？

☺ M: No, but I have always wanted to go.

沒有，但是我一直想去。

☺ W: It should be pretty fun.

那應該會很好玩。

☺ M: Be sure and bring me back a souvenir!

記得帶一個紀念品回來給我！

對話三

☺ M: Have you ever been up to see the president of the company?

你有沒有上樓去見過我們公司的總裁？

☺ W: No. Why do you ask?

沒有。你為什麼這麼問？

☺ M: John wants me to come up there with him for a meeting.

約翰要我跟他一起上去開會。

☺ W: Wow. Sounds like a big deal.

哇。聽起來好像很不得了。

☺ M: Well, our new project could be a big risk without investors.

嗯，我們的新計劃如果沒有投資人的話，將是一大冒險。

☺ W: Let me know what happens.

有什麼動靜要告訴我噢。

句型練習

1 Have you ever been to Italy?

你去過義大利嗎？

2 Have you ever been really late to work?

你曾經很遲去上班嗎？

3 Have you ever traveled outside the US?

你曾經到美國以外的地方去旅行嗎？

4 Have you ever been on a softball team?

你參加過壘球隊嗎？

基礎單字

✪ **vacation**		假期
✪ **company** [ˈkʌmpənɪ]		公司
✪ **office**		辦公室
✪ **islands** [ˈaɪləndz]		島嶼
✪ **souvenir** [ˌsuvəˈnɪr]		紀念品
✪ **president**		總裁
✪ **softball**		壘球

31 I've just had dinner.

我剛吃過晚餐

表示「才剛剛」做了某件事，也用現在完成式，不過要加上 just。例如：
I have just finished the work. 是說我「才剛剛」把工作做完。

對話一

☺ M: Do you want to go out and get some dinner?

你要不要去吃晚餐？

☺ W: No. I've just had dinner.

不。我剛吃過晚餐。

☺ M: Okay. We'll go some other time.

好的。我們改天再去。

☺ W: How about tomorrow?

明天怎麼樣？

☺ M: Sounds great!

很好！

第 5 章 完成式在會話的應用

☺ M: We've just seen the movie "Star Wars".

我們剛看過電影「星際大戰」。

☺ W: Did you like it?

你喜歡嗎？

☺ M: Yes. It was very entertaining.

喜歡。這部電影很有娛樂性。

☺ W: I am going to see it this weekend.

我這個週末要去看。

☺ M: I won't spoil it for you by talking about it.

我不談論它，以免破壞你的興致。

對話三

☺ W: How is John?

約翰好嗎？

☺ M: He's just finished his masters thesis.

他剛完成他的碩士論文。

☺ W: Wow! Is he excited?

哇！他很興奮嗎？

☺ M: I think so.

我想是的。

☺ W: He is probably wondering where he is going to find a job.

他可能正在想該到哪裡去找工作。

❶ He has just completed the assignment.

他剛把作業做完。

❷ I've just gotten to the point where I can speak English fluently.

我剛達到可以把英文講得很流利的地步。

❸ We've just been to that park.

我們剛去過那個公園。

❹ I've just called him.

我剛打過電話給他。

❺ I've just finished reading that book yesterday.

我昨天剛把那本書讀完。

基礎單字

❍ **entertaining** [ˌɛntɚˈtenɪŋ]	有趣的	
❍ **thesis** [ˈθisɪs]	論文	
❍ **spoil**	破壞興致	
❍ **complete**	完成	
❍ **assignment**	指定作業	
❍ **fluently** [ˈfluəntlɪ]	流利地	
❍ **point**	階段；程度	

32 I've already told him.

我已經告訴他了

　　文法名詞既然把「have+ 過去分詞」的形式稱為「完成式」,總是跟動作的完成有關吧?這句話雖然不錯,但是在實際英語會話中,要表示「已經」有某一回事,要多用一個 already 已經,否則就不一定表示動作的完成,例如:I have told him. 是「我告訴過他」,而 I have already told him. 才是「我已經告訴他了」。

對話一

☺ M: Does John know where the party is?

　　約翰知道宴會在哪裡舉行嗎?

☺ W: I've already told him.

　　我已經告訴過他了。

☺ M: Good. Is he bringing a date?

　　很好。他會帶伴來嗎?

☺ W: I did not ask.

　　我沒有問。

☺ M: I'll find out later.

　　我再問他好了。

對話二

☺ M: How is the report coming?

報告寫得怎麼樣了？

☺ W: I've already finished writing it.

我已經寫完了。

☺ M: Good. I look forward to reading it.

很好。我等待著要讀呢。

☺ W: I will put a copy on your desk Tuesday.

星期二我會放一份複本在你的桌上。

對話三

☺ M: Do you need any help?

可以為你們服務嗎？

☺ W: No. We've already seen what we were looking for.

不需要。我們已經看到我們要找的東西。

☺ M: If you need anything, let me know.

如果你們需要任何東西，就告訴我。

☺ W: Thank you.

謝謝你。

We will.

我們會的。

❶ I've already read that book.
那本書我已經讀過了。

❷ He has already talked to me.
他已經告訴我了。

❸ The car has already been fixed.
車子已經修好了。

❹ We've already been told where to go.
已經有人告訴我們該去哪裡了。

基礎單字

✪ **date**	同伴
✪ **report**	報告
✪ **already** [ɔl'rɛdɪ]	已經
✪ **copy**	副本
✪ **fixed**	修理好（**fix** 的過去分詞）

慣用語

✪ **find out**	找出答案
✪ **look forward to**	期待
✪ **look for**	尋找

33 A lot has happened since I last saw you.

從我上次見過你後，發生了很多事

對話一

☺ M: How have you been?

你最近怎麼樣？

☺ W: Good!

很好！

A lot has happened since I last saw you.

自從我上次見過你之後，發生很多事。

☺ M: What kind of stuff?

哪些事？

☺ W: I have an appointment right now, but I will call you tonight.

我現在有個約會，不過我今晚會打電話給你。

☺ M: Okay. I'll talk to you then.

好的。那時候我再跟你談。

對話二

☺ W: Have you been to Disneyland lately?

你最近有沒有去過迪士尼樂園？

☺ M: We have been there twice since they built the new roller coaster.

自從他們蓋新的雲霄飛車之後，我們已經去過兩次了。

☺ W: Do your kids like it?

你的孩子們喜歡嗎？

☺ M: They love it!

他們愛死了！

☺ W: I think we are going to go this weekend.

我想我們這個週末會去。

對話三

☺ M: Has John gone to China this year?

約翰今年去過中國了嗎？

☺ W: Yes. In fact, he has been in China since August 1.

是的。事實上，從八月一號開始他就在中國了。

☺ M: I did not know that.

我不知道這回事。

☺ W: He is running our office there.

他在負責我們在那裡的公司。

☺ M: I guess I have not been keeping up with things.

我想我的消息是不太靈通。

句型練習

① I've been working here since 198 ⑤

我從一九八五年就在這裡工作。

② I've been waiting for you since 7 o'clock.

我從七點開始就一直在等你。

③ I haven't seen John since Monday.

從星期一開始我就沒有看到約翰。

④ How long has it been since you had a vacation?

自從你上一次度假到現在，已經多久了？

⑤ It's been years since it snowed.

已經有好幾年沒有下雪了。

基礎單字

✪ since	自從
✪ happen	發生
✪ stuff [stʌf]	事情
✪ appointment	約會
✪ roller coaster [ˈrolɚ ˌkostɚ]	雲霄飛車
✪ run	管理
✪ snow	下雪

慣用語

✪ keep up with things	隨時注意最新動態
✪ in fact	事實上

34 He hasn't written me for two months.

他已經兩個月沒寫信給我

對話一

☺ M: How is John?

約翰怎麼樣？

☺ W: He hasn't written me for two months.

他已經有兩個月沒有寫信給我。

☺ M: I wonder what he is doing.

我不知道他在做什麼。

☺ W: I think he has been doing a lot of field work.

我想他在做很多實地考察的工作。

☺ M: He must be very busy.

他一定很忙。

對話二

☺ M: I have not been to the circus for many years.

我已經有好幾年沒看馬戲表演了。

☺ W: Me either.

我也是。

Wouldn't it be fun to go?

能去看馬戲的話，一定很好玩吧？

☺ M: That's what I was thinking.

我也是這麼想的。

☺ W: I will find out how much tickets are.

我去看看票價是多少。

對話三

☺ M: We haven't been able to take a vacation for a long time.

有好長的一段時間我們沒辦法休假。

☺ W: Are you going to take one this year?

今年你打算休假嗎？

☺ M: I do not know if we have the time.

我不知道我們是否有時間。

☺ W: You have to make the time.

你必須把時間硬擠出來。

☺ M: I would rather be able to retire early.

我寧願能夠早一點退休。

句型練習

❶ We haven't carried that brand for several months.

我們已經有好幾個月不賣那個品牌了。

❷ She has not been over here for weeks.

她已經有好幾個星期沒有過來這裡了。

❸ John hasn't been to school for days.

約翰有好幾天沒有去上學。

❹ I have not been able to log on to the network for a week now.

到現在為止已經有一個禮拜，我沒辦法上電腦。

❺ I've been skating for years.

我已經溜冰好幾年了。

基礎單字

○ **wonder** [ˈwʌndɚ]	想
○ **field** [fild]	實地；田野
○ **communicate** [kəˈmjunəˌket]	聯絡
○ **overseas**	海外
○ **circus** [ˈsɝkəs]	馬戲團
○ **ticket**	票
○ **retire**	退休
○ **brand** [brænd]	品牌
○ **skating**	溜冰

慣用語

○ **a lot of**	許多
○ **would rather**	寧願
○ **log on**	電腦上線

35 We haven't been to Disneyland yet.

我們還沒有去過迪士尼樂園

對話一

☺ M: We haven't been to Disneyland yet.

我們還沒有去過迪士尼樂園。

☺ W: You have to go.

你應該去。

It is a really good time for the kids.

小孩子會玩得很愉快。

☺ M: I think it is too expensive.

我認為太貴了。

☺ W: You can get coupons at the grocery store for discount tickets.

你可以在雜貨店拿到折價券，可以買折扣票。

☺ M: I will look into that.

我會注意看看。

☺ M: What is the status of your project?

你的案子目前進度如何？

☺ W: I have not written the conclusion yet.

我的結論還沒有寫。

☺ M: We need to have that by Friday.

我們星期五需要那一份案子。

☺ W: I will be sure that you have it by Thursday morning.

我保證到星期四早上，你就可以拿到。

☺ M: Good.

很好。

That's even better.

那樣更好。

對話三

☺ M: Has Mary called you?

瑪莉打電話給你了嗎？

☺ W: No. She has not talked to me yet.

沒有。她還沒有跟我說過話。

☺ M: She was supposed to ask you about the party tonight.

她原本是要問你有關今晚的宴會的事。

☺ W: What about it?

有什麼事嗎？

☺ M: I was wondering if it would be okay to bring my kids.

我在想是否可以帶小孩子來。

☺ W: No. It is an adult party.

不好。這是一個大人的宴會。

句型練習

❶ I haven't been able to find the file yet.

我還沒辦法找到那個檔案。

❷ Has it stopped raining yet?

雨停了嗎？

❸ She hasn't called me yet.

她還沒有打電話給我。

❹ He has not turned in his work yet.

他還沒有交他的功課。

❺ I haven't told them about the accident yet.

我還沒有告訴他們車禍的事。

✪ **status** [ˈstætəs]	情形	
✪ **conclusion** [kənˈkluʒən]	結論	
✪ **expensive** [ɪksˈpɛnsɪv]	昂貴的	
✪ **discount** [dɪsˈkaʊnt]	打折	
✪ **coupon** [ˈkupɑn]	折價券	
✪ **grocery store**	雜貨店	
✪ **adult**	大人	

慣用語

✪ **turn in**	交
✪ **look into**	查看

36 How long have you known Mary?

你認識瑪莉多久了？

對話一

☺ M: How long have you known Mary?

你認識瑪莉多久了？

☺ W: About 5 years.

差不多五年。

☺ M: Really?

真的嗎？

Did you go to school with her?

你跟她上同一所學校嗎？

☺ W: No. We worked together at TI.

沒有。我們一起在德州儀器公司上班。

☺ M: I did not know she was that old.

我不知道她年齡那麼大了。

☺ M: I am a little nervous about giving my speech tonight.

今天晚上我要演講，有一點緊張。

☺ W: How long has it been since you last gave one?

你上一次作演講到現在有多久了？

☺ M: About three years.

大約有三年。

☺ W: My goodness!

天啊！

I would be nervous, too.

如果是我，我也會緊張。

☺ M: I am about to go practice.

我要去練習了。

☺ W: Good luck!

祝你好運！

☺ M: How long has John worked for Acer?

約翰在宏碁上班多久了？

☺ W: I am not sure.

我不太確定。

Why?

怎麼啦？

☺ M: I have a friend who is looking for a job there.

我有一個朋友，想在那兒找工作。

☺ W: I have John's number if you need it.

我有約翰的電話號碼，如果你需要的話。

☺ M: No, thanks.

不，謝謝你。

I've already had it.

我已經有了。

句型練習

❶ How long have you been smoking?

你抽煙抽多久了？

❷ How long has he been studying English?

他學英文學多久了？

❸ How long has he been out of town?

他到外地去有多久了？

④ How long has he been on vacation?

他去度假有多久了？

⑤ How long have they been married?

他們結婚多久了？

基礎單字

☺ **nervous** [ˈnɝvəs]	緊張
☺ **practice**	練習

慣用語

☺ **out of town**	到外地去
☺ **on vacation**	去度假
☺ **Good luck!**	祝好運

37 I have been running for the last forty minutes.

過去的四十分鐘，我都在跑步

對話一

☺ M: You look tired.

你看起來很疲憊。

☺ W: I have been running for the last forty minutes.

過去的四十分鐘，我都在跑步。

☺ M: That sure is a long time!

那真的是很長的時間！

☺ W: I am training for a 10K race this weekend.

我為了這個週末的十公里賽跑在做練習。

☺ M: I am sure you will do great.

我確信你能夠做得很好。

對話二

☺ M: You seem tired.

你似乎很疲倦。

Have you been sleeping okay?

你最近睡得好嗎？

☺ W: No. My wife has been sick.

不好。我太太一直在生病。

☺ M: I am sorry to hear that.

我很遺憾聽到這件事。

☺ W: Thanks. She is getting better.

謝謝你。她已經好多了。

☺ M: Well, I hope you get some rest.

嗯，我希望你能多休息。

對話三

☺ M: How is the dinner coming?

晚餐做得怎麼樣了？

☺ W: Good, we have been cooking all day.

很好，我們一整天都在作菜。

☺ M: I can't wait to try the turkey.

我等不及要嚐嚐那隻火雞。

☺ W: It will be done in about thirty more minutes.

再三十分鐘就可以好了。

☺ M: Good. Do you need any help?

很好。你需要任何幫忙嗎？

☺ W: **No.** We have everything covered.

不需要。所有的事情我們都已經弄好了。

句型練習

❶ Have you been exercising lately?

你最近做運動嗎？

❷ I have been working on this project for weeks!

我好幾個星期一直在做這個計畫！

❸ Has she been coming to class on time?

她一直都準時來上課嗎？

❹ Has John been calling you with the updates?

約翰打過電話告訴你最新的資料嗎？

❺ You have been looking tired for weeks.

你已經有好幾個星期看起來都很疲倦。

基礎單字

✪ **tired**	疲倦的
✪ **race** [res]	賽跑
✪ **rest**	休息
✪ **turkey** ['tɝkɪ]	火雞
✪ **exercising** ['ɛksəˌsaɪzɪŋ]	做運動
✪ **lately**	最近
✪ **update** ['ʌp'det]	更新

38

When I arrived at the party, she had already left.

當我抵達宴會時，她已經離開了

對話一

☺ M: Did you see Mary last night?

昨天晚上你有沒有看到瑪莉？

☺ W: When I arrived at the party, she had already left.

當我抵達宴會時，她已經離開了。

☺ M: That's too bad.

那太可惜了。

☺ W: Why?

怎麼會呢？

☺ M: You didn't get to see her ridiculous witches costume.

你沒能看到她那荒謬的巫婆打扮。

☺ W: Hopefully I will get to see some of the pictures.

希望我能夠看到一些照片。

對話二

☺ M: Did you get to edit the report?

你有修改那一份報告嗎?

☺ W: No. John had turned it in before I could look at it.

沒有。在我有機會看之前,約翰就已經把它交出去了。

☺ M: I am going to have to talk to him about that.

我一定要跟他談談這件事。

☺ W: I'm not mad about it.

我並不生氣啊。

☺ M: I am upset.

我可很生氣。

He needs to be a team player.

他應該要有團隊精神。

句型練習

❶ When I got to the store, they had already closed.

當我到店裡時,他們已經關門了。

❷ The house was dirty. We hadn't cleaned it for weeks.

這個屋子很髒。我們已經有好幾個禮拜沒有清理了。

❸ When I arrived at the party, Mary had already gone home.

當我到宴會的時候，瑪莉已經回家了。

❹ I had just had lunch.

我剛吃過中飯。

❺ John had already left by the time I got there.

我到的時候，約翰已經離開了。

基礎單字

✪ **ridiculous** [rɪˈdɪkjələs]	荒謬的
✪ **witch**	巫婆
✪ **costume** [ˈkɑstjum]	服裝
✪ **edit**	修改
✪ **mad**	生氣
✪ **upset**	不高興

慣用語

✪ **be mad about**	對某事生氣

39 I used to play golf.

我以前打高爾夫球

對話一

☺ M: Do you play golf?

你打高爾夫球嗎？

☺ W: I used to play golf, but now I'm too lazy.

我以前打高爾夫球，但是現在我太懶了。

☺ M: That's too bad.

那可真不好。

☺ W: I was not very good anyway.

反正我也打不好。

☺ M: Well, if you ever want to go, let me know.

好吧，如果你想打的話，告訴我。

對話二

☺ M: John used to come to work early, but now he is always late.

約翰以前都很早來上班，但是他現在總是遲到。

☺ W: I wonder why.

我在想到底為什麼。

☺ M: I don't know.

我不知道。

I should probably ask.

我或許應該問他。

☺ W: He might think we are being nosy.

他可能會認為我們多管閒事。

☺ M: We are!

我們是多管閒事！

對話三

☺ M: We used to have a hammer around here.

我們以前有一把鐵鎚在這兒。

Have you seen it?

你有沒有看到？

☺ W: No, I have not.

沒有，我沒有看到。

☺ M: I guess we are going to have to buy a new one.

我想我們必須再買一把新的。

☺ W: We need to start storing things in one spot so we don't lose it.

我們需要開始把東西放在一個定點，才不會弄丟了。

☺ M: I know.

我知道。

I will make a list of where to put things.

我會列一張單子，說明我們要把東西放在哪裡。

句型練習

❶ She used to drive a Benz.

她以前開賓士車。

❷ I used to have a record player, but now I listen to CD's.

我以前有一個電唱機，但是現在我都是聽雷射唱片。

❸ We used to ride the bus to work.

我以前都是搭公車上班。

❹ John used to write me every week.

以前約翰每一個禮拜都寫信給我。

基礎單字

○ record player	電唱機
○ nosy ['nozɪ]	愛管閒事
○ hammer	鐵鎚
○ spot	地點

第 6 章

大膽的假設

40 If I didn't want to go, I wouldn't.

如果我不想去，我就不會去

對話一

☺ M: Where do you want to go for lunch?

你要去哪裡吃午飯？

☺ W: I have no idea.

我不知道。

☺ M: Do you think we would be gone too long if we went across town?

你想如果我們到市區的另一頭去，會不會太遠？

☺ W: Yes. Let's just grab a sandwich from across the street.

會。我們到對街去隨便買個三明治就好了。

☺ M: Sounds like a good idea.

聽起來是個好主意。

☺ M: Do you think I would look better if I got my hair cut short?

你想如果我把頭髮剪短，會不會好看一點？

☺ W: I don't know.

我不知道。

You have to decide those things for yourself.

你必須自己決定這些事情。

☺ M: I guess so.

我想也是。

☺ W: You look good now.

你現在看起來已經很好。

But I am sure you would look good with your hair short, too.

但是你如果把頭髮剪短，應該也會很好看。

句型練習

❶ I would go to the party if I were invited.

如果我受到邀請，我會去參加宴會。

❷ We would be in trouble if we did not go to the meeting.

如果我們沒去開會，我們會有麻煩。

❸ John would be upset if he did not get the award.

約翰如果沒有得獎的話，他會很生氣。

❹ Would you be late if I picked you up at 8:00 AM?

如果我早上八點來接你，你會不會遲到。

❺ What would happen if I did not go with you to the school?

如果我不跟你一起去學校會怎樣？

基礎單字

✪ **decide**	決定
✪ **grab** [græb]	匆忙地拿
✪ **sandwich**	三明治
✪ **across**	越過
✪ **award** [ə'wɔrd]	獎

慣用語

✪ **get the award**	得獎

41 I wish I knew the answer.

但願我知道答案

對話一

☺ M: How can John be late every day and not get in trouble?

約翰怎麼可能每天都遲到，而沒有惹麻煩？

☺ W: I wish I knew the answer.

但願我知道答案。

☺ M: Me too.

我也是。

☺ W: I guess the boss just does not notice.

我想老闆可能沒有注意。

☺ M: I am sure he would notice if I were late.

我確信如果我遲到的話，他一定會注意到。

對話二

☺ M: I wish I knew where I put those scissors.

但願我知道我把剪刀放那裡。

☺ W: When did you last have them?

你上一次使用是什麼時候？

☺ M: I used them yesterday on my pants.

我昨天用來剪我的褲子。

☺ W: I thought I saw them in the bathroom.

我想我在浴室有見到。

☺ M: I'll go and check.

我去看看。

對話三

☺ M: Can John come to the party?

約翰會來參加宴會嗎？

☺ W: He says he has other plans.

他說他有其他的事。

☺ M: Why is it that he always has plans?

為什麼他總是有其他的事？

☺ W: I don't know.

我不知道。

I wish I knew so I could tell you.

但願我知道，可以告訴你。

☺ M: I really don't care.

我真的不在乎。

I am just curious.

我只是是好奇而已。

句型練習

1 I wish I knew why Mary is so upset.
但願我知道瑪莉為什麼這麼生氣。

2 I wish I knew where to take Mary for dinner tonight.
但願我知道今天晚上該帶瑪莉去那裡晚餐。

3 I wish I knew how to ice skate.
但願我知道怎麼溜冰。

4 I wish I knew how to be more friendly.
但願我知道如何更友善一些。

基礎單字

○ **trouble** [ˈtrʌbl̩]	麻煩
○ **answer**	答案
○ **boss**	老闆
○ **notice** [ˈnotɪs]	注意
○ **scissors** [ˈsɪzɚz]	剪刀
○ **pants**	褲子
○ **bathroom**	浴室
○ **check**	查看
○ **curious**	好奇的
○ **friendly** [ˈfrɛndlɪ]	友善的

慣用語

○ **get in trouble**	遭到責罰

42 If~

要是……

對話一

☺ M: You missed the party last night.

昨天晚上你沒有來參加宴會。

☺ W: I was sick.

我病了。

☺ M: If I had known you were sick, I wouldn't have told John to expect you.

如果我知道你生病了，我就不會叫約翰等你。

☺ W: I am sorry, but I forgot to call you.

對不起，但是我忘了打電話給你。

☺ M: It's no big deal.

沒有什麼大不了。

I hope you get better.

我希望你好多了。

☺ M: I thought John was supposed to come to the meeting.

我以為約翰會來參加會議。

☺ W: I don't think he knew.

我不認為他知道。

☺ M: I may have forgotten to tell him.

我可能忘記告訴他。

☺ W: If he had known about the meeting, he would not have missed it.

如果他知道要開會的話,他不會不來的。

☺ M: I will have to tell the boss it is my fault.

我會告訴老闆,那是我的錯。

對話三

☺ M: John has been having problems with Jane not doing her part of the work.

約翰一直對珍不做她應做的部分感到忿忿不平。

☺ W: I know.

我知道。

She has been leaving it all to him.

她向來都把所有的事情留給他。

☺ M: If you had known about the problem, why didn't you tell me?

如果你知道這個問題，為何沒有告訴我？

☺ W: It is none of my business.

那不關我的事。

☺ M: We all need to work together to work efficiently.

我們應該一起解決問題，這樣工作才有效率。

☺ W: I'm sorry.

很抱歉。

Next time I will let you know.

下一次我會讓你知道。

句型練習

❶ If we had known about the change, we would have been on time.

如果我們早知道時間變更了，我們就會準時到達的。

❷ If John had been to Disneyland, he wouldn't have asked you if he should go or not.

如果約翰去過迪士尼樂園的話，他就不會問你他是否應該去了。

❸ If I had known about your problem, I wouldn't have blamed you for your poor performance.

如果我早知道你的問題，我就不會責怪你工作表現不好。

④ If I had known you were married, I wouldn't have asked you out.

如果我早知道你結婚了，我就不會邀你出去。

基礎單字

○ **expect** [ɪksˈpɛkt]	等候
○ **meeting**	會議
○ **miss**	錯過
○ **efficiently** [əˈfɪʃəntlɪ]	有效率的
○ **change**	改變
○ **performance** [pəˈfɔrməns]	表現
○ **blame**	責怪

慣用語

○ **none of my business**	沒我的事
○ **on time**	準時
○ **next time**	下一次

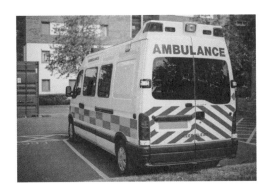

43 I wish I had come earlier.

我要是早一點來就好了

對話一

☺ M: This place is crowded.

這個地方很擁擠。

☺ W: I wish I had come earlier.

我要是早一點來就好了。

☺ M: It was just as crowded when the store opened.

店一開門，就這麼擁擠了。

☺ W: It might be worth coming back after the sale is over.

或許等拍賣過後再來，還是值得的。

☺ M: I think I might do the same.

我想我也會這麼做。

對話二

☺ M: Can you hear that car alarm?

你聽見汽車警報器嗎？

☺ W: Yes! I wish it would stop ringing.

聽見！我希望它不要再響了。

☺ M: I am about to go and knock on the owner's door.

我忍不住要過去敲那車子主人的門。

☺ W: I don't even think he is home.

我想他根本不在家。

☺ M: I wish there was something we could do.

我希望我們有辦法可以想。

對話三

☺ M: I wish I had been able to see Star Wars when it first came out.

要是星際大戰一出來的時候我就能去看，那該多好。

☺ W: It was a good movie, but you were better off not being in the crowded theater.

那是一部好看電影，但是你不到那擁擠的戲院去，還是好些。

☺ M: I think the crowd adds to the experience.

我認為人群可以增加經驗。

☺ W: I guess we are different.

我想我們兩人不同。

I hate the crowds.

我不喜歡人潮。

① I wish I had been at your graduation ceremony.

我希望我有去參加你的畢業典禮。

② I wish I had planned better for this meeting with the investors.

要是這個跟投資者的會議，我計畫得更充分就好了。

③ I sure wish I had been able to go with my parents to Europe.

要是能跟我父母去歐洲，那該多好。

④ I wish I had learned Spanish in school.

要是我在學校的時候學過西班牙文就好了。

⑤ I wish I had been allowed to see the report before you turned it in.

我多麼希望在你把報告交出去之前，我能看看。

基礎單字

☺ **crowded** [ˈkraʊdɪd]		擁擠的
☺ **earlier**		早一點
☺ **sale**		拍賣
☺ **alarm** [əˈlɑrm]		警報器
☺ **knock** [nɑk]		敲
☺ **theater** [ˈθɪətɚ]		戲院

☺ **experience**	經驗
☺ **crowd**	人群
☺ **graduation** [ˌɡrædʒʊˈeʃən]	畢業
☺ **ceremony** [ˈsɛrəˌmonɪ]	典禮

慣用語

☺ **graduation ceremony**	畢業典禮
☺ **came out**	上映

44 I wish you wouldn't drive so fast.

我希望你不要開這麼快

對話一

☺ **M:** Are you nervous?

你很緊張嗎？

☺ **W:** A little.

有一點。

I wish you wouldn't drive so fast.

我希望你不要開那麼快。

☺ **M:** I want to get to the meeting on time.

我想要準時到達會議。

☺ **W:** I want to get to the meeting alive!

我想要能活著到達會議。

☺ **M:** Okay, I'll slow down.

好吧！我會慢下來。

☺ M: This restaurant has terrible service!

這家餐廳的服務真差！

☺ W: Maybe they are shorthanded tonight.

或許今天晚上他們缺乏人手。

☺ M: Maybe so, but I wish they wouldn't make it our problem.

或許是如此。但是我希望他們不會讓這件事造成我們的困擾。

☺ W: I am sure they are not doing it on purpose.

我確信他們不是故意這麼做的。

They probably don't want to lose their business.

可能他們只是不願失去上門的生意。

☺ M: I know.

我知道。

I need to be more patient.

我需要更有耐心一些。

對話三

☺ M: I wish the table next to us would quit smoking.

我多麼希望我們鄰桌的人不要再抽煙。

☺ W: Why don't you ask?

你為什麼不要求他們呢？

☺ M: I don't want to be rude.

我不願顯得很莽撞。

☺ W: Then you have no right to complain.

那麼你就沒有抱怨的權利。

☺ M: Okay, I'll ask politely.

好吧！我會很客氣地請求他們。

句型練習

❶ Don't you wish they had better service here?

你不希望他們這裡有好一點的服務嗎？

❷ I wish the boss wouldn't complain so much.

我希望老闆不要抱怨那麼多。

❸ I wish I didn't speak English so poorly.

我希望我的英文不要講得那麼糟。

❹ I wish you wouldn't talk so loud.

我希望你不要講得那麼大聲。

❺ I wish she wouldn't be so nosy.

我希望她不要那麼愛管閒事。

基礎單字

☺ **nervous**	緊張的
☺ **service** ['sɜvɪs]	服務
☺ **alive**	活的
☺ **terrible** ['tɛrəbl̩]	口語糟透的
☺ **restaurant**	餐廳
☺ **patient** ['peʃənt]	有耐心的
☺ **quit**	停止
☺ **right**	權力
☺ **complain** [kəm'plen]	抱怨
☺ **rude**	不禮貌
☺ **nosy**	愛管閒事
☺ **loud**	大聲的

慣用語

☺ **on purpose**	故意的
☺ **slow down**	慢下來
☺ **on time**	準時

45 How many cars are involved in the accident?

這件事故有幾部車子牽連在內？

對話一

☺ M: The radio says there is a car wreck blocking the highway.

收音機說有一場車禍，把高速公路都堵住了。

☺ W: How many cars are involved in the accident?

這場車禍有幾部車子牽連在內？

☺ M: The report didn't say.

報導沒有說。

☺ W: I guess we will have to take the back road home.

我想我們必須要抄小路回家。

對話二

☺ M: I wonder if I can bring food to the meeting.

我在想，我是否可以帶食物來開會。

☺ W: I don't think that is allowed.

我想那是不行的。

☺ M: I have seen John bring food before.

我曾經看見約翰帶過食物來。

☺ W: I am pretty sure John got reprimanded for it.

我蠻確定，約翰為了那件事遭到譴責。

☺ M: I guess I will skip lunch then.

那我想我只好不吃午飯了。

句型練習

❶ How long until dinner is done?

晚餐還有多久才會做好？

❷ John and I are worn out.

約翰和我都累壞了。

❸ Who is invited to the party?

有那些人受到邀請來參加宴會？

❹ We are allowed only three sick days per year.

我們每年只有三天的病假。

☺ **radio**	收音機
☺ **wreck** [rɛk]	車禍
☺ **blocking** [ˈblɑkɪŋ]	堵塞
☺ **highway**	高速公路
☺ **involved** [ɪnˈvɑlvd]	牽連
☺ **report**	報告
☺ **reprimanded** [rɛprɪˈmændɪd]	斥責；譴責
☺ **skip**	略過

慣用語

☺ **be worn out**	累壞了
☺ **sick days**	病假
☺ **skip lunch**	不吃午飯
☺ **back road**	小路

46 The house wasn't damaged by the storm.

房屋沒有遭暴風雨毀損

對話一

☺ **M:** Did you get rained on last night?

昨天晚上你們那裡有沒有下雨？

☺ **W:** Yes. We had quite a storm.

有，我們這裡有一場很大的暴風雨。

☺ **M:** How is your house?

你們的房屋還好吧？

☺ **W:** The house wasn't damaged by the storm.

房屋沒有被暴風雨損壞。

☺ **M:** That's good.

那很好。

Storm damage can be very expensive.

暴風雨的毀損，修復可是很貴的。

☺ M: I would like to go to Disneyland.

我想要去迪士尼樂園。

☺ W: Me too.

我也是。

I was kept from going last year by an overseas assignment for work.

我去年因被派到海外工作,導致不能去。

☺ M: Maybe we can go together.

或許我們可以一起去。

☺ W: That would be fun.

那一定很有趣。

☺ M: I'll see when I can get off from work.

那我看看我什麼時候可以請假。

☺ W: Let me know what you hear.

你得到消息後,讓我知道。

☺ M: Did you see John today?

你今天有沒有看見約翰?

☺ W: No. His store was closed.

沒有,他的店關著。

☺ M: I wonder why.

我不知道為什麼？

☺ W: I think one of his kids was sick.

我想他有一個小孩病了。

句型練習

❶ The building wasn't affected by the power outage.

這棟大樓沒有被停電所影響。

❷ The bank was closed yesterday.

銀行昨天關門。

❸ They weren't told what time to wake up.

沒有人告訴他們，什麼時候該起床。

❹ They weren't open for the holiday.

他們假日不營業。

基礎單字

✿ **storm**	暴風雨
✿ **damaged** [ˈdæmɪdʒd]	遭到破壞
✿ **damage**	損壞
✿ **expensive**	昂貴的
✿ **overseas** [ˈovɚˈsiz]	海外

⊘ **affected** [əˈfɛktɪd]	受影響
⊘ **building**	大樓
⊘ **outage** [ˈaʊtɪdʒ]	水、電、煤氣等中斷；停

慣用語

⊘ **power outage**	停電
⊘ **last year**	去年
⊘ **get off from work**	請假

第 7 章

英語會話
常用被動式

47 The Olympics will be held in Atlanta.

奧林匹克運動會將在亞特蘭大舉行

☺ M: The Olympics will be held in Atlanta this year.

奧林匹克運動會，今年將在亞特蘭大舉行。

☺ W: It seems like it would be too hot there.

那裡似乎太熱了吧。

☺ M: I think the ocean moderates the climate.

我認為海洋會調節氣候。

☺ W: I don't know.

那可說不定。

I think it just makes it humid.

我認為海洋只會使天氣更悶溼。

☺ M: Well, the games are going to be there regardless.

是嘛，無論如何這場運動會一定會在那裡舉行。

對話二

☺ M: I'd like to know when the hotel renovations will be completed.

我想要知道旅館的整修什麼時候會做完。

☺ W: They will be completed in two days.

他們兩天內會完成。

And the hotel will open the day after.

旅館會在隔一天開門。

☺ M: Are you taking reservations now?

你們現在接受預訂房間嗎？

☺ W: Yes, we are.

是的，我們接受預訂。

Let me transfer your call.

讓我把你的電話轉過去。

句型練習

❶ The store will be closed Saturday.

這家店星期六不營業。

❷ John will be gone Friday.

約翰星期五會離開。

❸ I shall be gone all of next week.

下個禮拜我都不在。

④ She will be allowed to watch TV after her homework is done.

她要等到家庭作業做完，才可以看電視。

⑤ The door will be locked at 8:00 p.m.

這道門在下午八點會上鎖。

基礎單字

○ **moderate** ['mɑdə,ret]		緩和
○ **climate** ['klaɪmɪt]		氣候
○ **completed** [kəm'plitɪd]		完成了
○ **renovations** [,rɛnə'veʃənz]		整修
○ **transfer** ['trænsfə]		轉
○ **regardless** [rɪ'gɑrd,lɪs]		無論如何
○ **humid** ['hjumɪd]		潮濕

48 Are you being helped, sir?

先生，有人服務您嗎？

對話一

☺ M: Are you being helped, sir?

先生，有人服務您嗎？

☺ W: Yes, thank you.

有的，謝謝你。

☺ M: If you need anything else, ask any one of us.

如果你需要其他什麼東西，可以問我們其中任何一個。

☺ W: Actually, I would like to try these shoes on in a size 10.

事實上，我要試穿十號的這種鞋子。

☺ M: I'll get those right away.

我馬上去拿。

☺ M: My name is John Lin.

我的名字是林約翰。

I have a reservation for a single.

我預訂一間單人房。

☺ W: Yes, we have you in room 205.

是的，我們有你的登記，在 205 房間。

But the room is being cleaned right now.

但是房間現在正在清理。

It won't be ready until three o'clock.

要到三點才能準備好。

☺ M: That's okay.

沒關係。

I'll come back later.

我待會再回來。

句型練習

❶ The room is being cleaned right now.

房間現在正在清理。

❷ Look at those old houses. They are being knocked down.

看看那些老房子，他們正被拆除著。

❸ The elevator is being repaired.

電梯現在正在修理

❹ Are you being helped, ma'am?

小姐，有人為您服務了嗎？

基礎單字

○ **reservation** [rɛzɚˈveʃən]	預定
○ **single**	單人房
○ **elevator** [ˈɛlə͵vetɚ]	電梯
○ **repaired**	修理

慣用語

○ **try on**	試穿
○ **knocked down**	拆除

49 I haven't been invited.

我沒有受到邀請

MP3
50

對話一

☺ M: Are you going to the party?

你要去參加宴會嗎？

☺ W: I haven't been invited.

我沒有受到邀請。

☺ M: I am inviting you.

我現在就邀請你。

☺ W: I am going then.

那麼我就去。

對話二

☺ M: John hasn't been allowed to come to work in days.

約翰已經好幾天不能來上班。

☺ W: I wonder if he is okay.

我在想他是否還好。

☺ M: Actually, I think he is on sick leave.

事實上，我想他是請病假。

☺ W: The flu has been going around lately.

最近流行感冒正在流行著。

☺ M: I am glad I had my shot earlier this year.

我很慶幸今年稍早我去打了預防針。

對話三

☺ M: We haven't been allowed to see the report since Thursday.

自從星期四之後，我們就不許看那份報告。

☺ W: Why is that?

為什麼呢？

☺ M: John says he is adding classified information.

約翰說他正在加入一些機密資料。

☺ W: They talk all about teamwork.

他們這樣還敢一直強調什麼團隊工作。

☺ M: I know.

我知道。

I feel the same way.

我也有這種感覺。

❶ The horse hasn't been ridden for weeks.

這匹馬已經好久沒騎了。

❷ She has been stricken since her grandfather died.

自從她的祖父去世後，她就很悲傷。

❸ We haven't been helped yet.

還沒有人為我們服務。

❹ I haven't been asked for my opinion in a long time.

好久沒有人問我的意見了。

基礎單字

✪ **actually** [ˈæktʃʊəlɪ]		事實上
✪ **flu**		感冒
✪ **shot**		注射
✪ **classified** [ˈklæsɪfaɪd]		機密的
✪ **stricken** [ˈstrɪkən]		悲痛的
✪ **opinion**		意見

慣用語

✪ **on sick leave**	請病假

50 The car should have been fixed yesterday.

車子昨天就該修好了

MP3 51

對話一

☺ M: I am here to pick up my car.
我來這裡取我的車子。

☺ W: It is not ready yet.
車子還沒有好。

☺ M: The car should have been fixed yesterday.
車子昨天就該修理好的。

☺ W: We had to wait on a part to come in.
我們在等一個零件進來。

☺ M: I wish you had called and told me.
我但願你們打了電話通知我。

☺ W: I apologize for the inconvenience.
我很抱歉造成你的不便。

☺ M: Did John bring you the report?

約翰把報告拿給你了嗎？

☺ W: I don't think he is here today.

我想他今天沒有來。

☺ M: Really?!

真的嗎？

He should have been talked to by someone.

應該有人跟他好好談一談才行。

☺ W: I have not seen him.

我一直都沒有看到他。

☺ M: I will ask around.

我會到處問看看。

句型練習

❶ I should have been included on the guest list.

客人名單上應該包括我。

❷ I would have been stuck in traffic if I had taken the highway.

如果我走高速公路的話，我可能會陷在交通堵塞裡。

❸ We could have been luckier and won the lottery.

我們可能會更幸運一些，贏得彩券的。

❹ The air conditioner should have been turned on this morning.

冷氣機今天早上就該開了。

基礎單字

✿ **apologize** [əˈpɑləˌdʒaɪz]	道歉
✿ **inconvenience** [ˌɪnkənˈvinjəns]	不方便
✿ **part**	零件
✿ **lottery** [ˈlɑtərɪ]	彩券
✿ **air conditioner**	冷氣機

慣用語

✿ **wait on**	等著
✿ **in front of**	在～之前
✿ **ask around**	到處問
✿ **guest list**	客人名單
✿ **turn on**	開

51 The problem can be solved.

這個問題可以解決

對話一

☺ M: I cannot figure out this problem.

我沒辦法解決這個問題。

☺ W: The problem can be solved with a little work.

這個問題需要一些小技巧,就能解決。

☺ M: Would you mind showing me how?

你可以告訴我怎麼做嗎?

☺ W: Sure.

可以。

Let me just finish sending this e-mail.

讓我先把這個電子郵件寄出去。

對話二

☺ M: How long will this paper take to do?

這份報告要多久才能做完？

☺ W: I think it can be completed in a day.

我想一天就可以做完了。

☺ M: Great.

很好。

Let me know when you are finished.

你做完之後，讓我知道。

☺ W: Okay.

好的。

I will also bring you a copy of the document.

我還會帶一份影印本給你。

對話三

☺ M: What do you think about the TWA crash investigation?

TWA 航空公司的飛機撞毀的調查，你認為怎麼樣？

☺ W: I think the mystery will be solved in about a month.

我認為這個謎可以在一個月內得到解決。

☺ M: Why such a long time?

為什麼要這麼長的時間？

☺ W: The North Atlantic coast has a lot of rough weather.

北大西洋海岸的氣候很不好。

☺ M: That is a good point.

你說得有道理。

句型練習

❶ The car can be fixed without spending a lot of money.

這部車子不需要花很多錢，就可以修好。

❷ The meeting will be held without the chairman being there.

這個會議將會在主席不在的情況下召開。

❸ I can be annoyed easily by crowds and traffic.

我很容易被人群和繁忙的交通所激怒。

❹ We can be included in the list if you need us.

如果你需要我們的話，可以把我們列入名單上。

基礎單字

☺ **mind**	介意
☺ **copy**	副本
☺ **document** [ˈdɑkjəˌment]	文件
☺ **crash** [kræʃ]	飛機等的撞毀
☺ **investigation** [ɪnˌvɛstəˈgeʃən]	調查
☺ **coast**	海岸
☺ **rough**	不平靜的
☺ **weather**	氣候
☺ **include** [ɪnˈklud]	包括
☺ **annoyed** [əˈnɔɪd]	惱怒的

慣用語

☺ **figure out**	想出答案

52 I want to be left alone.

我想要一人獨處

對話一

☺ M: How are you feeling?

妳現在覺得怎麼樣？

☺ W: I want to be left alone.

我想要一人獨處，不要別人打擾。

☺ M: If there is anything you want to talk about, I don't mind listening.

如果妳有什麼事情想談一談，我不介意當妳的聽眾。

☺ W: No. I really just do not feel well.

不用了。我真的覺得很不舒服。

對話二

☺ M: What has Mary been up to?

瑪莉近來怎麼了？

☺ W: She wants to be promoted at work.

她想要在工作上得到升遷。

☺ M: So she has been working quite a lot.

所以她就一直拼命工作。

☺ W: That would be an understatement.

這樣講還不足以形容。

對話三

☺ M: I want to be included in the training schedule.

在訓練表上把我也包含進去。

☺ W: I am sorry, but the list is full.

對不起，只是名單都已經滿了。

☺ M: Who can I talk to about an exception?

我應該找誰談，才可以破例？

☺ W: You will have to talk to your division head.

你必須要找你們的部門經理談。

句型練習

❶ Do you want to be on our softball team?

你要參加我們的壘球隊嗎？

❷ I need to be on the guest list to tomorrow's dinner.

明天晚上晚宴的客人名單也要列上我的名字。

❸ We need to be allowed to work overtime.

我們應該被允許加班。

❹ I want to be able to work late.

我希望能夠工作到晚一點。

❺ She wants to be accepted as part of the team.

她想要被接受成為團隊的一員。

基礎單字

✪ **understatement**	所述尚不足以形容
✪ **promoted** [prə'motɪd]	被擢升
✪ **head**	主管
✪ **exception** [ɪk'sɛpʃən]	例外
✪ **division** [də'vɪʒən]	部門
✪ **overtime**	加班

53 John got fired from his job.

約翰遭到解聘

對話一

☺ M: John got fired from his job.

約翰被解聘了。

☺ W: It is about time.

也該是時候了。

☺ M: Why do you say that?

你為什麼這麼說呢？

☺ W: He was late to work every day.

他每天上班都遲到。

☺ M: Maybe it is best then.

那或許解雇了最好。

對話二

☺ M: We got released from the training class early.

我們的訓練課提早結束。

☺ W: What did you do with your extra time?

你多出來的時間做什麼事呢？

☺ M: I came back to work and finished my report for the week.

我回來上班，把這個禮拜的報告做完。

☺ W: You are such a dedicated worker.

你上班可真認真。

☺ M: Thank you.

謝謝你。

對話三

☺ M: Have you seen Mary?

你看見瑪莉嗎？

☺ W: Mary got transferred to Thailand.

瑪莉被調到泰國去了。

☺ M: You're kidding!

你在開玩笑吧！

I hadn't heard.

我沒聽說呀。

☺ W: Yes. She is opening our new office over there.

真的。她要在那裡給我們公司開辦一間新的分公司。

句型練習

❶ John got dismissed from class today.

約翰今天的課提早結束。

② I got promoted last week.

我上個禮拜被擢升。

③ I got paid for all of my travel expenses.

他們付我所有出差的費用。

④ She got reprimanded for her bad behavior.

她因為行為不佳而受到責罵。

基礎單字

✪ **dismissed** [dɪsˈmɪst]	（形）解散
✪ **behavior** [bɪˈhevjɚ]	行為
✪ **expense** [ɪksˈpɛns]	費用
✪ **extra** [ˈɛkstrə]	額外的
✪ **dedicated** [ˈdɛdɪˌketɪd]	一心一意的
✪ **transferred** [ˈtrænsfɚd]	調動

慣用語

✪ **got fired**	被解雇
✪ **got transferred to**	被調到
✪ **got dismissed from class**	下課
✪ **were let out of the class**	下課
✪ **got paid for**	被付給
✪ **got reprimanded for**	被責備

54 You should have your hair cut.

你應該把頭髮剪短

對話一

☺ M: I need a new look.

我需要一付新造型。

☺ W: I think you should have your hair cut.

我想你應該把頭髮剪短。

☺ M: I don't know.

我拿不定主意。

I am afraid to cut it.

我很怕把它剪短。

☺ W: Why?

為什麼？

☺ M: It takes so long to grow back.

那要花好長時間才能夠再留長。

☺ W: You have got to take some risk!

你總得冒一點險嘛！

對話二

☺ M: I need to have my air conditioning fixed.

我得把我的冷氣機修好。

☺ W: Do you have a repairman already?

你找好修理工人了嗎？

☺ M: No. I need to find one.

沒有。我需要找一個。

☺ W: My brother has his own company if you are interested.

如果你有興趣的話，我哥哥有一個自己的公司。

☺ M: That sounds great.

那很好。

When you get a chance, give me his card.

有機會請你把他的名片給我。

對話三

☺ M: I need to get my drivers license renewed.

我需要換我的駕駛執照了。

☺ W: That is always such a pain in the neck.

那是很麻煩的事情。

☺ M: I know.

我知道。

I dread going.

想到去換我就怕。

☺ W: I wonder why you can't do it by mail anymore.

我搞不懂為什麼不能以郵寄的方式換取駕照。

☺ M: They had a lot of problems with fraud.

因為有人詐騙，他們遇到很多麻煩。

句型練習

❶ I think you should have your pants hemmed.

我認為你應該把你褲子的折邊縫好。

❷ I think we should have our house cleaned.

我認為我們應該把我們的房子清理乾淨。

❸ I need to get my shirts pressed.

我得把我的襯衫燙一燙。

❹ We need to get our reports printed.

咱們須要把報告印出來。

❺ I think you should have your paper checked by the secretary.

我認為你應該讓秘書檢查一下你的報告。

基礎單字

☺ **look**	外表
☺ **risk**	冒險
☺ **air conditioning**	冷氣系統
☺ **repairman** [rɪ'pɛrmən]	修理工人
☺ **own**	擁有
☺ **company** ['kʌmpənɪ]	公司
☺ **card**	名片
☺ **renewed** [rɪ'njud]	駕駛執照換新
☺ **neck**	脖子
☺ **dread** [drɛd]	畏懼
☺ **fraud** [frɔd]	（名詞）詐騙
☺ **hemmed**	縫褶邊
☺ **pressed**	用熨斗燙
☺ **secretary** ['sɛkrə,tɛrɪ]	秘書

慣用語

☺ **grow back**	頭髮長回來
☺ **pain in the neck**	（口語）非常麻煩

第 8 章

英語會話
慣用法

55 I saw her go out a minute ago.

我才剛看見她走出去

對話一

☺ M: Where is Mary?

瑪莉在哪裡？

☺ W: I saw her go out a minute ago.

一分鐘之前，我才看見她出去。

☺ M: When she comes back, have her call me.

她回來的時候，叫她打電話給我。

☺ W: Do you want me to look for her?

你要我去找她嗎？

☺ M: No. It is not that important.

不用了。不是很重要的事情。

對話二

☺ W: What's wrong, John?

約翰，怎麼啦？

☺ M: I can hear the fire bell ring next door.

我聽得到隔壁的火警警鈴在響。

☺ W: I don't hear it.

我沒聽見吶。

☺ M: I have sensitive hearing.

我的聽覺很敏銳。

☺ W: Well, if it bothers you, I can check into it.

是嗎，如果這個警鈴使你覺得很煩，我可以去看看怎麼回事。

☺ M: Please do.

請你去查一下吧。

對話三

☺ M: I can feel the wind blow through the window.

我可以感覺到風從窗戶吹進來。

☺ W: Would you like me to shut it?

你要我把它關起來嗎？

☺ M: No, it feels good.

不用，這種感覺很好。

☺ W: I like to let in the Spring air sometimes.

我偶而喜歡讓春天的空氣進來。

☺ M: Yes. It is very refreshing.

是的。這種空氣很清新。

句型練習

1 I can see the water drip from the ceiling.
我可以看到水從天花板滴下來。

2 I can feel the air conditioning blow.
我可以感覺到冷氣在吹。

3 I can hear the motor run.
我可以聽到引擎在轉著。

4 I saw her come in a while back.
剛剛不久前我才看到她進來。

5 I heard him walk by a minute ago.
一分鐘之前，我才剛聽見他從這兒走過。

基礎單字

○ **ring**	鈴響
○ **important**	重要的
○ **blow** [blo]	吹
○ **shut**	關閉
○ **refreshing** [rɪˈfrɛʃɪŋ]	清爽的
○ **drip**	滴水
○ **motor**	馬達

慣用語

○ **fire bell**	火警警鈴
○ **next door**	隔壁
○ **check into**	查看

56 Can you smell something burning?

你聞到東西燒焦嗎？

對話一

☺ M: Can you smell something burning?
你聞到東西燒焦嗎？

☺ W: Yes. I wonder where it is from.
是的，我不知道焦味是從那裡來的。

☺ M: I think it is from next door.
我想是從隔壁來的。

☺ W: I will go over there and find out.
我過去那裡看一看怎麼回事。

對話二

☺ M: Do you see someone trying to open that door across the street?
有人正試著打開對街那一家的門，你看見沒有？

☺ W: No. Where are they at?
沒有，在那裡？

☺ M: Just to the right of the restaurant.
就在那家餐廳的右邊。

☺ W: Do you think we should call the police?

你想咱們應該打電話給警察嗎？

☺ M: I think that would be a good idea.

我想那是一個好主意。

對話三

☺ M: Do you hear something rattling when I start the car?

當我發動車子的時候，你有沒有聽到鏗鏗卡卡的聲音？

☺ W: Yes. It sounds strange.

有，聽起來很奇怪。

☺ M: The mechanic says it is my brakes doing an auto check of themselves.

修車師傅說，那是我車子的剎車在做自動檢查。

☺ W: That sounded pretty loud.

聽起來非常大聲。

☺ M: I think I am going to get a second opinion.

我想我還會找第二家修車廠問意見。

句型練習

❶ Can you feel something blowing down the hall?

你有沒有感覺有東西從走廊吹過來？

② Can you see something glowing in the closet?

你有沒有看到壁櫥裡有東西在發光？

③ Can you smell popcorn cooking?

你有沒有聞到爆米花在爆的味道？

④ Do you hear a motor running?

你有沒有聽到引擎在轉的聲音？

⑤ Can you hear someone yelling?

你有沒有聽到有人在喊叫？

基礎單字

✿ **burning** [ˈbɝnɪŋ]	燃燒著
✿ **police**	警察
✿ **rattling** [ˈrætl̩ɪŋ]	短而且尖銳的聲音
✿ **mechanic**	汽車技工
✿ **brake**	剎車
✿ **glowing** [ˈɡloɪŋ]	發光
✿ **closet**	壁櫥
✿ **popcorn**	爆米花
✿ **yelling** [ˈjɛlɪŋ]	喊叫

慣用語

✿ **find out**	找出事實

57 I can't make him come.

我請不動他來

MP3
58

對話一

☺ M: Do you want John to come to your graduation?

妳要約翰來參加妳的畢業典禮嗎？

☺ W: I can't make him come.

我請不動他來。

But I would like him to be there.

但我很想要他出席。

☺ M: I will send him an invitation.

我來寄一張邀請卡給他。

☺ W: Good.

很好。

I think it will be a lot of fun.

我想大家一定玩得很愉快。

☺ M: You can't let John forget to take his lunch to work tomorrow.

明天你可別讓約翰忘記帶午飯去上班。

☺ W: I try to remind him in the morning.

每天早上我都試著提醒他。

But he still forgets.

但他還是會忘記。

☺ M: Put his keys in the lunch sack.

把他的車鑰匙放在午餐袋裡。

☺ W: That is a good idea.

這主意不錯。

☺ M: I hope it works.

我希望這樣做有效。

I can't afford to take him out to lunch anymore!

我再也負擔不起帶他到外頭去吃午餐了！

句型練習

❶ I can't make the rock move.

我搬不動這個石頭。

❷ I can't let you take the report home without your promise that no one else will read it.

如果你不保證沒人會看這份報告的話，我就不能讓你帶它回家。

❸ He can't have the report modified without permission.

沒有得到允許，他不得修改這份報告。

❹ We can't let the reporter make our political decisions for us.

我們不能讓記者替我們做政治決定。

基礎單字

○ **graduation** [,grædʒʊ'eʃən]		畢業
○ **invitation**		邀請卡
○ **remind** [rɪ'maɪnd]		提醒
○ **sack**		紙袋
○ **rock**		岩石
○ **promise** ['prɑmɪs]		答應；保證
○ **modified** ['mɑdə,faɪd]		更改
○ **permission** [pɚ'mɪʃən]		許可
○ **political** [pə'lɪtɪkl]		政治的
○ **decision**		決定

58 I can't imagine you riding a motorcycle.

我無法想像你騎摩托車的樣子

對話一

☺ M: I got my new motorcycle yesterday!

我昨天拿到我的新摩托車！

☺ W: I can't imagine you riding a motorcycle.

我無法想像你騎摩托車的樣子

☺ M: I have been riding them since I was fifteen years old.

我從十五歲就開始騎了。

☺ W: Are they fun to ride?

騎摩托車很好玩嗎？

☺ M: Oh yes!

噢，是的！

They are a lot of fun.

非常好玩。

☺ M: How are you doing at your new job?

妳的新工作做得怎麼樣？

☺ W: I am doing great.

我做得很好。

☺ M: Do you miss the old job?

妳懷念妳的舊工作嗎？

☺ W: I can't miss working for so little money.

我不可能懷念薪水那麼低的工作。

☺ M: I can't stop thinking about vacation.

我沒辦法不去想度假的事。

☺ W: Where are you going?

你要去那裡度假？

☺ M: France!

法國！

☺ W: Wow!

哇！

How long are you going to be gone?

你要去多少？

☺ M: I will be gone for three weeks.

我會去三個星期。

句型練習

1 I can't finish eating all of this ice cream.

我吃不完這些冰淇淋。

2 I won't stop asking you to come to the party until you say yes.

除非你答應，否則我不會停止要求你參加宴會。

3 I can't imagine working for such a big company.

我無法想像替這一間大公司做事的情形。

4 I can't finish running a marathon, so I don't plan to enter one.

我不可能跑完馬拉松賽跑，所以我不計劃參加。

5 I can't keep walking to work every day.

我不能再每天走路去上班。

基礎單字

○ **motorcycle** [ˈmotəˌsaɪkl̩]	摩托車	
○ **riding**	騎（**ride** 的現在分詞）	
○ **imagine** [ɪˈmædʒɪn]	想像	
○ **fun**	樂趣	
○ **miss**	想念	
○ **ice cream**	冰淇淋	
○ **marathon** [ˈmærəˌθɑn]	馬拉松賽跑	

59 May I borrow your car?

我可以借用你的汽車嗎？

對話一

☺ A: May I borrow your car?

我可以借你的汽車用嗎？

☺ B: It depends.

那要看情形。

What do you need it for?

你要車幹什麼？

☺ A: I forgot my lunch.

我忘了帶午飯。

I want to go out and get a sandwich.

我想要出去買個三明治。

☺ B: All right and get me a burger, okay?

好吧，也幫我買個漢堡，好嗎？

☺ A: Sure, no problem.

當然可以，沒問題。

☺ A: May I have Wednesday off?

星期三我可以請假嗎？

☺ B: What for?

要做什麼？

☺ A: I'd like to take a personal day.

我想請一天事假。

☺ B: We are busy this week.

這個禮拜我們很忙。

Could you take a day off next week?

你下禮拜再請假可以嗎？

☺ A: I guess so.

我想可以吧。

☺ B: Great.

那好。

What day of next week?

下禮拜的那一天？

☺ A: How about Monday?

星期一，可以嗎？

1. May I come in?
   我可以進來嗎？
2. May I speak to John?
   我可以跟約翰講話嗎？
3. May I have a word with you?
   我可以私下跟你談談嗎？。
4. May I borrow your typewriter?
   我可以借你的打字機用嗎？
5. You may smoke if you like.
   如果你想抽煙的話，你可以抽。

基礎單字

✪ **depend** [dɪˈpɛnd]		視～而定
✪ **burger**		漢堡
✪ **typewriter** [ˈtaɪpˌraɪtɚ]		打字機
✪ **smoke**		抽煙

慣用語

✪ **come in**		進來
✪ **take a personal day**		請事假

60 I may fly to Hong Kong next Tuesday.

下禮拜二我可能會飛到香港

對話一

☺ A: Please cancel my afternoon appointments.

請你把我下午的約會取消掉。

☺ B: Are you going out to lunch?

你要出去吃午飯嗎？

☺ A: No, but I may need to go home early.

不，不過我得早一點回家。

☺ B: What's wrong?

有事嗎？

☺ A: Nothing.

沒什麼。

I just need some rest.

我只是要休息一下。

對話二

☺ A: I may be late tonight, so don't wait up.

今天晚上我可能會晚一點回來，所以不用等我。

☺ B: Where are you going?

你要去那裡？

☺ A: I have a meeting, remember?

我有個會要開，記得嗎？

☺ B: Oh, that's right.

噢，是啊。

How late will you be?

你會多晚回來？

☺ A: I should be home by 11:00, but you never know.

我應該十一點會回到家，但是很難說。

對話三

☺ A: I may change my major.

我可能會轉系。

☺ B: Don't you like medicine?

你不喜歡醫學嗎？

☺ A: It's interesting.

醫學是很有趣。

But I think computer science is where my interests lie.

但是我想計算機科學才是我的興趣所在。

☺ B: Well, I hope you know what you are doing.

是嗎，我希望你知道你在做什麼。

句型練習

1 I may go to France.

我可能去法國。

2 Mary may not come to the party tonight.

今天晚上瑪莉可能不會來參加宴會。

3 It may rain this afternoon.

今天下午可能會下雨。

4 My parents may come to the States this summer.

今年夏天我父母可能會到美國來。

5 He may not pass the exam.

他可能通不過考試。

基礎單字

✪ **fly**		搭機前往
✪ **cancel** [ˈkænsl̩]		取消
✪ **remember** [rɪˈmɛmbɚ]		記得
✪ **major**		主修
✪ **medicine** [ˈmɛdəsn̩]		醫學；醫藥
✪ **interesting**		有趣的
✪ **interest**		興趣

慣用語

✪ **wait up**	熬夜等人

每天5分鐘,流利英語一本通

英語系列：54

作者／施孝昌
出版者／哈福企業有限公司
地址／新北市板橋區五權街16號
電話／(02) 2808-6545　傳真／(02) 2808-6545
郵政劃撥／31598840　戶名／哈福企業有限公司
出版日期／2019年2月
定價／NT$ 299元 (附MP3)

全球華文國際市場總代理／采舍國際有限公司
地址／新北市中和區中山路2段366巷10號3樓
電話／(02) 8245-8786　傳真／(02) 8245-8718
網址／www.silkbook.com 新絲路華文網

香港澳門總經銷／和平圖書有限公司
地址／香港柴灣嘉業街12號百樂門大廈17樓
電話／(852) 2804-6687　傳真／(852) 2804-6409
定價／港幣100元 (附MP3)

email／haanet68@Gmail.com
網址／Haa-net.com
facebook／Haa-net 哈福網路商城

圖片／shutterstock

Copyright © 2019 HAFU Co., Ltd.
著作權所有　翻印必究
如有破損或裝訂缺頁，請寄回本公司更換

Origenal copyright © Talk a lot in English

國家圖書館出版品預行編目資料

每天5分鐘,流利英語一本通 / 施孝昌著. --
新北市：哈福企業, 2019.2
　面；　公分. -- (英語系列；54)

ISBN 978-986-97425-0-4(平裝附光碟片)

1.英語 2.讀本

805.188

哈福